"Shh," Kay whispered to the baby.

She started moving again, not sure which way to go.

A noise to the right startled her. The play of light and dark in the woods confused her. Was she still moving away from her assailant?

Then a large shadow stepped out from behind a tree, and she ran into a solid, muscular body.

He gripped her arms with an ironclad hold. When she yelled for help, baby Kaleb bawled. Her assailant yanked on Kaleb, but he was secured against her in the baby carrier. The brute jerked harder.

As they struggled, Kay kicked the man's shin. He couldn't take her child. She poured all her energy into protecting Kaleb.

When she scanned the darkness surrounding her, she suddenly didn't see her assailant.

"Kay, I'm here!" Drake shouted. "Are y'all okay?"

All the tension in her body siphoned from her. Now she was. "Yes."

Drake clicked on a flashlight and swept the area with the bright beam, then stepped next to her. "He's gone. You and the baby are safe now."

For now.

Margaret Daley, an award-winning author of ninety books (five million sold worldwide), has been married for over forty years and is a firm believer in romance and love. When she isn't traveling, she's writing love stories, often with a suspense thread, and corralling her three cats, who think they rule her household. To find out more about Margaret, visit her website at margaretdaley.com.

Visit the Author Profile page at Harlequin.com for more titles.

LONE STAR CHRISTMAS RESCUE

MARGARET DALEY

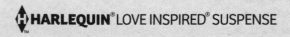

Recycling programs
for this product may
not exist in your area.

LOVE INSPIRED BOOKS

ISBN-13: 978-0-373-67858-7

Lone Star Christmas Rescue

Copyright © 2017 by Margaret Daley

www.Harlequin.com

Printed in U.S.A.

Yea, though I walk through the valley of the shadow of death, I will fear no evil; For You are with me; Your rod and Your staff, they comfort me.
—Psalms 23:4

To my granddaughters

ONE

Texas Ranger Drake Jackson hiked to the edge of the cliff and stared at the raw beauty stretching out before him. Not far away was the Rio Grande and Mexico. The case he'd been assigned involved a human smuggling ring that worked both ways—trafficking people both into and out of the United States. One of their corridors had recently been rumored to be along this part of the border in his territory, but every time the task force got close, someone ended up dead and the route disappeared.

If only they could catch a break.

A vision of his younger sister materialized in his mind. Smiling. Laughing at something he'd said. But that was fifteen years ago, before she vanished without a trace. At that time, he'd been a Texas highway patrol officer and had taken vacation days to work the case. But he could never find her. In his gut, and based on the evidence he'd gathered, Drake knew she'd become a victim of a human trafficking ring. Even now, he and his family lived in limbo concerning Beth.

He shook the image from his thoughts. He might not be able to bring Beth back, but he was determined to stop others from ending up like her. He knew firsthand what it was like for a family to have no resolution for a loved one's fate.

With a sigh, he turned away from the cliff's edge. A faint cry from below caught his attention. A wounded animal? Again, the sound drifted to him. A cat—cougar?

He lifted his binoculars and scanned Big Bend National Park's rugged terrain below for the source of the noise. The cries grew to wails, allowing him to home in on the source. He sucked in a sharp breath. Nestled between large boulders sat a baby, tugging on the shirt of a woman sprawled on the ground. The location was an odd place for anyone to be. Quickly he checked the surrounding area. He didn't see anyone nearby. Returning his attention to the lady, he noticed she wasn't moving or reacting to the crying baby next to her. Something was wrong.

He shrugged off his backpack and dug into it for the rope and gear he used for rappelling. It would take two or three times longer for him to hike down to the canyon. If the woman was injured, she might need help right away. After putting in his anchors, setting up his rigging and double-checking all the equipment, Drake stepped off the cliff with his backpack. Facing the rock facade, he walked down it at a sixty-degree angle.

The baby's continuous bawling urged him to move as fast as he could. Drake kept looking over his shoulder at the pair below. When his feet hit the bottom, he unhooked himself, then hurried the few yards to the woman and child. By the time he reached them, the little boy's face was beet red, tears running down his cheeks. Dressed in jeans, a dirty long-sleeved white shirt and tennis shoes, the lady beside the child appeared as though she was taking a nap—no obvious signs of an injury.

Drake knelt next to the child and stroked his hand up and down the baby's back. "Shh. I'm here to help," he said in a soft voice and removed a water bottle to offer the little boy a few sips.

As he continued to pat the child, he turned his attention to the woman, relieved to see her chest rising and falling with each breath. When he felt for her pulse on the side of her neck, its racing beat didn't surprise him.

The baby, probably no more than six or seven months old, calmed down and looked at Drake with big brown eyes and long black lashes. Assessing him.

"You aren't alone." He wished he could ask the child what had happened and get an answer.

What was wrong with the young woman? Why was she out here with a baby and no backpack—or water?

Heatstroke? He touched her smooth, soft skin, pinkish from the sun but not badly sunburned. He ran his fingertips over her forehead, her flesh sweaty but not hot enough to indicate heatstroke. He breathed a little easier—although it wouldn't take long for her to become dehydrated, and then her body would shut down.

Drake leaned down and said in a firm voice, "Wake up, ma'am." He gently shook her shoulder.

No response.

After another glance down the front of her body, he returned his attention to her face, with long light brown hair framing it. Still no obvious sign of why she wasn't responding. He hated to stop soothing the baby, but he needed to find out why the lady was unconscious.

The baby whimpered the second he removed his hand so he could roll the woman over to check her back for any injuries. He locked gazes with the little boy for a few seconds, saying, "It's okay. I'm still here," before he shifted his focus to the unresponsive lady.

He immediately saw what was wrong. Blood

matted her hair and stained the ground below her head. Had she fallen or had someone hit her? He surveyed the area. Unless someone was hiding behind the rocks, they were the only people in the canyon. He carefully examined the wound—about four inches long but hard to tell how deep.

As the baby watched him, Drake grabbed his backpack and pulled out his first aid kit. He treated the injury and wrapped gauze around her head to stem the flow of blood. From the amount of it, uncoagulated, soaking into the ground, she'd been hurt recently. He laid the woman on her back again with her face turned to the side, revealing her bandage. Her eyelids fluttered open.

"I'm a Texas Ranger. I'm here to help. What happened?" he asked, but not before she'd closed her eyes again. "Ma'am, I'm here to help you and the baby."

Nothing.

With no cell reception, he'd have to hike out of the canyon and head for the nearest park road, which was closer than circling the cliffs and making his way to his car. He couldn't leave her or the baby alone while he did. He'd have to carry them both to the highway. She needed medical help as soon as possible.

He put his first aid kit away, then took a bottle and drank a long sip before he held the baby and offered him more water. He drank, the liquid running down his chin and neck. After that, Drake quickly fashioned a carrier for the little boy using his backpack with most of his gear removed. After giving him another sip of water, Drake strapped him in, covered the top of the child's head and then shrugged into the makeshift baby hauler.

The boy's giggles brought a smile to Drake's face. Hopefully, he thought it was a game. He glanced over his shoulders into those big dark eyes. Was the woman his mother? There weren't too many similarities between them. "This is the way to travel. Let someone else do the walking."

The baby babbled in response.

Drake drew in a deep breath, squatted and gently scooped the injured lady—no more than five feet three inches—into his arms and then stood. As he trudged across the canyon floor, he kept visually sweeping the terrain for any sign of someone else. Occasionally he looked at the slender-built woman or peered over his shoulder at the little boy who had fallen asleep against his back after only ten minutes.

When Drake emerged from the canyon, he knew a paved road was only about a mile away. He thought about stopping and resting, but instead he paused and used a boulder to prop the woman—heavier than he'd expected—against it so he could get the bottle out and take a gulp of water. The child slept through the maneuvering. Resuming his hike, Drake shoved away the burning sensation in his arms and shoulders and kept going. The woman might be small, but she had a muscular build.

In the distance, he spied a truck on the highway, but it was too far for him to flag down. He increased his speed. Five hundred yards away, another vehicle drove by heading west. Sweat rolled down his face as he began to jog, not wanting to miss another ride. He struggled to drag in enough oxygen to fuel his body and to keep the woman cradled against his chest safely.

One hundred yards.

Catching sight of a white car approaching from the east, he accelerated his pace as much as he could without jostling the injured lady too much. He was within twenty yards when the SUV flew by, not slowing down. Drake continued toward the road that led to the Panther Junction Visitor Center, but at a walk. His mad dash to flag down the vehicle had awakened the baby and left Drake panting, his arms burning even more from the strain.

He slanted a look at the little boy, whose mouth turned down. "Someone will come soon."

The baby jabbered back at him, any evidence of a frown gone.

Drake guessed he liked the sound of his voice,

so as he strode along the highway in the direction of the visitor center, he spoke softly about the animals he'd seen in Big Bend National Park. When he started telling the child about the mountain lion he'd seen in the spring, he looked down at the lady in his arms. Her eyes, dark like the baby's, stared at him.

"You're okay. I'm Drake Jackson. I'm taking you to get medical assistance. I found you passed out."

Her forehead furrowed, and she winced. "My head—hurts."

"You've been unconscious since I discovered you almost an hour ago. What's your name?"

Pain flittered across her face. Her eyelids began to slide shut. "I—"

Staring at her closed eyes, he murmured, "Ma'am?"

A sense of urgency slithered down his spine. She needed help now, and he wished he had a fast way to get it.

The baby whined.

"She'll be all right. We're only a few miles away from the visitor center," he said in a singsong voice, hoping to calm the little boy while in the heat of the desert wondering if he had the stamina to make it before it was too late. At least it was the first of December and cooler than other times in the park along the border with Mexico.

A sound drew his attention, and he zeroed in on a red sedan coming toward him. Unable to wave the driver down, Drake moved into the center of the road, praying he would stop and take them back the way the vehicle had come.

The car pulled onto the shoulder. The window slid down, and an older woman in the passenger seat asked, "Do you need help?"

"Yes." Drake glanced down at the hiker in his arms. "She needs medical attention as quickly as possible. Can you take us to the Panther Junction Visitor Center?"

"Of course we can. Get in." The older woman exited the vehicle. "I can hold the child." After she unstrapped the little boy from the carrier on Drake's back, she opened the rear door for him and then returned to the front seat with the baby.

Carefully he slipped into the back seat, adjusting the injured lady in his lap.

The driver made a U-turn and said, "I'm Clarence Moore, and this is my wife, Susan."

"I'm Texas Ranger Drake Jackson. I found this wounded woman and the baby alone in a canyon."

"Do you want some water?" Susan asked while the child drank from a plastic bottle.

"Yes, ma'am. I'd appreciate it."

Susan bent forward and grabbed another water bottle, then passed it to Drake. "We came prepared with our own."

"Thanks. That's always a good idea in Big Bend." He took a deep swig of the cold liquid, relishing it as it slid down his parched throat.

His gaze locked onto the injured woman's open brown eyes. "Do you want some?"

"Yes," she answered in a slow rasp.

Drake's arm, tingling from numbness, held her torso up at an angle. Shifting to relieve that sensation, he assisted her in taking a drink. A flowery aroma mingling with the scents of sweat and dust wafted to him. He was thankful she was short and didn't weigh much over 110 pounds, but he hadn't been sure how much farther he could have carried her without taking a break.

When she finished drinking, he swallowed another gulp, the whole time watching her as she peered at him. Assessing him, much like the baby had. On closer scrutiny, she and the child looked similar, more than he'd originally thought.

"Who are you?" he asked again. *Why did you have a young baby out in the middle of nowhere?*

A frown marred her attractive features. "I don't know."

* * *

Running. Gasping for air. Clutching a baby close. Images bounced around in her mind, then suddenly vanished. Her eyes popped open to a dimly lit strange place. She lay in a bed hooked up to monitors nearby.

Panic—danger swamped her. She had to get out of here.

She sat up. The room tilted and spun. She collapsed back onto the bed, closing her eyes to stop the swirling. Her stomach roiled. All she wanted to do was surrender to the darkness lurking close, but fear held her in the here and now.

Where am I?

Who am I?

A sound penetrated through her mounting alarm. Footsteps.

She couldn't shake the sense of danger. She opened her eyes again and frantically searched for a button to push for help.

"How are you doing, ma'am?" a deep male voice asked in a Texan drawl.

A vaguely familiar tall, large man, dressed in tan slacks and a white cowboy hat, stood only a few feet away. Her attention riveted on the silver star pinned to his long-sleeved white shirt. Police? Why was he here? Her head pounding, she grappled for the call button and pushed it while scrambling to the far side of the bed, the railing trapping her where she was. That sensation skyrocketed her distress.

"Who are you?" she asked in a quavering voice. Where had she seen him before? Confusion greeted that silent question.

He smiled, two dimples appearing on his tanned face. "I'm Texas Ranger Drake Jackson. I found you in Big Bend National Park yesterday afternoon."

"Alone?" escaped her mouth. An image of him leaning over her flashed into her mind. The picture vanished as quickly as it had appeared. Why did she think they hadn't been alone?

"No. Do you know your name?"

The dream that woke her up materialized in her mind. A baby in her arms? Sun beating down on them? Bright lights shining in her face? People around her? Was that real or her imagination?

"Did I have a baby with me?"

"Yes. Can you tell me your name? I'd like to contact your next of kin."

She had a baby with her. Did she have a husband? She rubbed the place where a wedding ring should be if she was married. Nothing. "I—I don't know my name."

His blue eyes dimmed. "What do you remember?"

Before she could answer, an older nurse entered her room. "I'm glad to see you're awake.

I'll contact the doctor. In the meantime, do you need anything, miss?" The nurse approached her bed on the opposite side of the Texas Ranger, checked her vitals, then shined a bright light into her eyes.

She delved into her mind, trying to recall anything that would lead to her identity and why she was in the hospital. But all she encountered was a blank slate, as though she'd never existed until now. "Where are my clothes?" Maybe they would indicate who she was.

The nurse crossed to a closet and withdrew a paper sack. "Everything you had with you is in here. Do you want to go through it?"

"Yes, please." When she reached for the bag, her hand shook. Awareness of the large man on her other side, watching her, caused her to clutch the paper bag and quickly draw it to her chest, feeling what little was inside. Was this all she had of her past?

She bowed her head and squeezed her eyes closed, desperate for any memory of who she was. She pictured herself standing on a mountaintop, scanning the valley below. Where was she? She couldn't tell. Was it a real place or merely her imagination?

A void held her, like an insect in amber. Caged. She felt empty, with no past to tell her who she was. The sensation of being in the middle of an ocean with only miles and miles of water surrounding her flooded her mind. Nothing for as far as she could see.

Her heartbeat raced, and her breathing shortened until she panted for each swallow of air.

"Miss, are you all right?" the nurse asked while the Texas Ranger moved closer.

His nearness surprisingly didn't frighten her. Instead, it comforted her as she sucked in gulps of the oxygen-rich air. She couldn't lose it. That wouldn't help her find out what happened. "I'll—be—okay," she managed to say between gasps.

Another minute passed before she felt in control of her breathing. She needed to talk alone with the Texas Ranger about how he found her. Maybe that would help her remember.

And she needed to find out about the baby from her dreams. She couldn't remember being a mother or married, but then, she couldn't remember anything of her past.

She turned her attention to the nurse. "I'd like to talk to the doctor whenever he comes."

"I'll let him know."

"Thanks." She waited until the nurse left the room before swinging her gaze back to the intensity in Drake Jackson's blue eyes, totally focused on her. Strangely, she didn't feel intimidated.

"How did you find me? You said I had a baby with me. Where is he?"

One eyebrow rose. "You know it's a boy. Do you know his name?"

Why had she said *he*? It just came out. "No. I can't remember anything."

"Your fingerprints were taken and run through the system, but nothing has come up yet."

Instead of disappointment that they couldn't ID her, relief fluttered through her. "I should be thankful. That means I haven't been in trouble with the law, at least."

He chuckled. "Fingerprints are on file from other sources beside the criminal system."

The soft sound of his laughter warmed her, making her feel less alone.

"To answer your questions about where the baby is, he's in the hospital, too."

She sat up straight, this time without the room swirling. "He's hurt?"

"Dehydrated, like you. He'll be released soon."

"Then what?"

"That depends on you. The state will take charge if you can't show he's yours. We'll run a search for Baby Doe's identity."

"Don't!" she said before she could stop herself.

TWO

"*Don't*? Do you know how he came to be in your possession?" Drake inched closer to the woman's hospital bed. His earlier impression of her had been fear and confusion, both understandable if her memory was affected by her injury. Or was that a ruse? What if she'd kidnapped the baby and come up with an amnesia cover story to delay an explanation? "Why don't you want to know the child's identity?"

"I—I do, but..." She looked away, staring at the door. "I can't shake the feeling something's wrong here."

"Like what?"

Her gaze locked with his. "I don't know." She fumbled with her sack of belongings, clasping it against her chest.

The anguish in her voice sounded genuine. As a Texas Ranger, Drake had to consider all angles of a situation. He'd seen a lot in his fifteen years working in law enforcement. If he couldn't remember who he was or what had happened, he would feel the same way. He wanted to believe her but… "Maybe your clothing will help you remember something." People with a traumatic brain injury could suffer total or partial amnesia that could be permanent or temporary. He didn't think she was faking, but he couldn't completely dismiss that possibility.

She unrolled the top of the paper bag and glanced inside. For a long moment, she remained quiet, then she slowly reached inside and pulled out her dirty white shirt. Next came the jeans, socks and shoes. She checked every pocket and withdrew money from the front one. After she counted the three hundred dollars, she murmured, "I have this but no ID. Why?"

Instead of finding any answers, Drake only discovered more questions. "I don't know. Is that all in the sack?"

"That's all." She turned the bag upside down, and a gold necklace plopped onto her blanket. Her eyes grew wide. "I didn't see that."

Drake started to reach for the piece of jewelry, stopped and brought his arm back to his side. His gaze latched on to a letter carved into the oval locket. "I think it opens."

With trembling hands, she picked up the delicate chain and palmed the golden ornament. With her stare fixed on it, she slowly opened it and gasped. "I think this may be a photo of me. Is it?" She touched her face as though her fingers could discern the answer by feel. She passed the necklace to him, her forehead scrunched.

She continued to shake, and all he wanted to do was comfort and reassure her everything would be all right. But he couldn't. He had no idea what was going on. He had to remain detached, professional.

How did she know what she looked like if she couldn't remember who she was? Slowly he examined the two photos in the locket. "This is you, and the picture of the baby is the same little boy you had with you."

"So I must be his mother." A quaver flowed through each word.

"Probably. You're connected somehow. How did you know what you look like?"

"I…" She shook her head slowly. "I remember dreaming of this baby and me being in trouble."

He studied the pictures, then the woman he'd rescued. He saw similarities between them, but the child's coloring was darker, possibly of Hispanic descent. "What trouble?"

She closed her eyes, her head dropping forward.

Had she lost consciousness again? Or was she pretending?

Her eyes suddenly opened wide. "Right before

I woke up, I remembered a vague image of me running with him clutched in my arms."

"Why were you running?"

Her large brown eyes, filled with bewilderment, lifted to his. "I don't know."

"Does the photo of the baby spark any other memories?"

"No, but maybe if I see him, it will."

"I'll let the nursing staff know. He's still being given fluids through an IV."

"What hospital am I in?"

"Cactus Grove Hospital."

She frowned.

"Does Cactus Grove, Texas, sound familiar to you?"

"No. Is this where you live?"

"Yes, outside town on a family ranch. Cactus Grove, along Interstate 10, has about forty thousand residents." He gave the necklace back to the woman. "Does the engraved letter *K* on the locket mean anything to you? The initial of your first name?"

She fiddled with the piece of jewelry, rubbing her thumb over the letter. "Not sure. Maybe?"

"Or your last name?"

She shook her head. "No idea, but I guess until I figure out who I am, I'd rather go by a name that might be mine."

"Kay?" He spelled the word out.

She nodded.

"How about the baby?"

"Maybe when I see him and hold him, I'll remember something."

"Let me check if you can as soon as possible. I'll talk with the head nurse." He walked toward the door.

"You're leaving?" Her voice cracked on the last word.

The sound shivered down him, and again he found himself wondering what it would feel like not remembering who you were—alone, everyone a stranger. "Only to talk with Rosa Martinez. I'll be right back."

In the hallway, Drake quickly located the head nurse and requested the baby be brought to Kay when possible.

The nurse glanced at the door to Kay's room. "She remembered her name?"

"Not exactly, but the locket she'd been wearing had an engraved *K* on it and two photos inside—one of Baby Doe and the other of the woman I brought in."

"I like the name. I have an aunt Kay. It sounds like she might be the child's mother after all. Seeing her baby might help with her memory. I'll check on the little boy and personally bring him to Kay as soon as possible. After the doctor

deals with an emergency, he'll be here to check Baby Doe for possible release later today."

"Thanks." As Drake made his way back to the hospital room, his cell phone rang. Noticing it was from the El Paso Texas Rangers headquarters, he quickly answered it. "Jackson here. What's up?"

"The park ranger at Big Bend National Park called. A murdered couple has been found."

"And he wants us to handle the case rather than the FBI or their own investigators?" He'd rather stay and be here for Kay. She didn't have anyone else.

"It was Park Ranger Calhoun who asked for you."

The guy he'd dealt with after bringing Kay to the ranger's station at the park. "Is this tied to the woman I rescued?"

"Possibly. The couple killed was Clarence and Susan Moore."

A chill streaked down his spine. "Tell him I'm on my way." Now he had to tell Kay he was leaving. He knocked, then pushed open the door.

As he entered, she glanced his way. "Will she bring the baby to me?"

"Yes, as soon as possible."

Kay—having a name felt so much more normal to him—wadded the blanket in her fists. "I've been trying to remember while you were gone. Nothing. Now I'm not even sure about what I thought I dreamed. I tried to picture that last image, and I can't."

She looked lost. He hated to leave. "I never recall my dreams after I wake up." He cleared his throat. "I have to leave for a while."

"I was hoping you could be here when I see the baby."

"I wish I could, but—" he left his card on the bedside table "—the nurse is waiting on the doctor to check the little boy. If you need to talk with me, call me. There will be times the cell reception won't be good, but leave a message and I'll call back when I can. I should be able to return by early evening."

"That long?"

"It's important, or I wouldn't leave." He didn't want to tell her anything else. The couple's murder very likely didn't have anything to do with Kay—at least he hoped. She didn't need to worry about that on top of all she had to deal with. He turned to leave, stopped and looked back at her, so alone in the hospital bed. "I'm here to help you."

She smiled, her eyes brightening for a few seconds. "Thank you."

When he left the room, the urge to remain stayed with him the whole way to his car. But a stronger pull drew him back to Big Bend.

* * *

With her eyes closed, a dull pain throbbing against her temples, Kay reclined at a sixty-degree angle in the hospital bed, trying to recall anything that could help her remember who she was. Memories had been stripped from her mind as though this were the day she'd been born.

A few minutes ago, she'd known how to do things like walk into the bathroom and wash her face. She even brushed her teeth and relished the peppermint flavor. She could read the label on the toothpaste, and when she went back into the main part of the room, she noticed it was two o'clock.

So why can't I remember my name? Where I live? How I ended up in the park—with my child?

Still, no answers flooded her.

She slid farther under the top sheet and blanket, wishing she could pull it up over her and hide under the covers. The sound of the door opening caused her to tense each time she heard it. When the head nurse entered the room, cradling a baby against her, Kay exhaled her held breath. At least Rosa Martinez wasn't another stranger coming in. There had been a parade of them in the past hours when all she wanted to see was the Texas Ranger or the baby found with her. Kay hoped she could find some answers to all the questions swirling around in her head.

"The doctor is releasing Baby Doe later today," Nurse Martinez said, stopping next to her bed.

"To who?" Kay asked as she peeked at the dark-haired little boy.

"That depends on what the State decides. A case worker will be here around five."

Case worker? How was she going to prove she was the child's mother? Would the photos in the locket be enough?

"Do you want to hold him?"

"Yes." Kay sat up, her heartbeat pounding as she waited to take the child, who cooed and smiled at her. Did the baby know her?

When Kay settled the little boy against her, she knew it hadn't been the first time. The baby reached up and explored Kay's face, continuing to grin, his eyes bright, as though he was used to touching Kay and interacting with her.

"I see he knows you. I'll leave you two to get reacquainted. If you need me, just push the button."

"Thanks," Kay said, her attention riveted to the boy's adorable oval face, his sun-kissed skin, as the head nurse left the room. "How are you, sweetie? I wish I remembered your name. I can't call you Baby Doe."

The child babbled, with "Mama" the only recognizable sound in the string.

Mama. Kay's throat tightened with conflicting emotions—from awe to fear—that she'd tried to hold at bay. How was she going to take care of this child when she didn't know who she was? Three hundred dollars wouldn't go far. If she was this child's mother, then where was the father? Kay held up her left hand, staring at her third finger, which gave no indication she'd worn a wedding ring recently. On her right middle finger, she wore an opal one.

Suddenly more questions deluged her. Was she divorced? Or widowed? What if she never married the father of—again she stared at the baby, willing a name to pop into her head.

Kevin? Kyle? No! Another name surged to the foreground. "Kaleb," Kay said out loud, and the little boy giggled, touching Kay's mouth. "Is Kaleb your name?"

The little boy caught sight of the hospital ID bracelet around his wrist and began playing with it.

Kay sighed. *If only you could talk.* The child's reaction to the name confirmed what Kay would call him until she discovered otherwise. Kaleb.

The past hours' exertion crept through Kay's body. Her headache kept demanding her attention, but she refused to let it get in the way of her time with Kaleb. Kay lounged back and cuddled the baby against her while he played with her curls. The feeling of Kaleb's fingers combing through her hair stirred a protective instinct—not an unfamiliar feeling.

She hugged Kaleb. "Sweetie, I won't let anything happen to you."

The door swung open, and suddenly a man appeared in her room. A dark-complexioned stranger. Large. Scowling. Her heartbeat went from calm to racing in seconds. She tightened her hold on Kaleb and picked up the call button. The scent of cigarette smoke wafted to her, nauseating her.

His thick dark eyebrows slashed downward. "Amy Grafton?"

"No," she said with as much force as she could without shouting. If he came another foot closer, she would call for help.

He took a step toward her bed. "But this is room 236."

She pressed the button, then clutched both arms around Kaleb, who had grown quiet, as though the baby felt all of her tension. "A nurse is coming. I'm not Amy." What if she was? No, she didn't think she was, and she didn't like the man's body language, as if he was preparing for a fight, his gaze darting about as though he was searching for something.

Rosa Martinez swung the door open and nearly hit him with it. A tall orderly stood behind the head nurse.

The stranger pivoted. "Sorry, ma'am. Wrong room." Then the large man rushed from her room so fast he shoved the nurse against the door and nearly knocked the orderly over.

Rosa frowned and peered into the hallway before dismissing the orderly and heading toward Kay.

"Should I call security?" The nurse stopped next to the bed with her eye on the entrance into the room.

"He was looking for someone called Amy Grafton."

"He was? I'm not familiar with a patient by that name on this floor. Maybe she's still in ER, and they haven't brought her up to her room yet."

A niggling sensation told Kay that wasn't the case. Chills swathed her from head to toe.

"What did you need? Did Baby Doe spark any memories?"

"He responded to me and the name Kaleb."

Rosa grinned. "That's great."

"I want to keep him in here for the time being. Is that okay?"

"It's not normal protocol, but I'll talk with the doctor and see if he'll okay it. In the meantime, enjoy Kaleb. I hope that's his name. It's beautiful."

Kay hoped so, too. That meant she was beginning to remember her past. "Thanks."

When the head nurse left her alone, Kay whipped back the sheets, her attention fixed on the door, her legs dangling off the side of the bed. "I don't have a good feeling about that man." The fear she'd tried to tamp down exploded, driving Kay into motion. "Kaleb, we're leaving."

The intense sun beat down on Drake as he examined the crime scene at Big Bend National Park. A hiker had found the bodies of Clarence and Susan Moore—what was left of them. Drake had seen his share of dead people, but the sight before him churned his gut. This retired couple had helped him when he'd needed it. If at all possible, he wouldn't let their deaths go unsolved.

"As you see, they were tortured," the park ranger, Don Calhoun, said, "and from the condition of the bodies, not long after they left the visitor's center yesterday."

After bringing him and Kay to it. "Why tortured? Has anything like this happened recently in the area?"

"No. That and the connection to what happened with the lady made me decide to call you in on this."

Was this connected to Kay somehow? "I appreciate being notified. I'd like to help with the investigation."

Don combed his fingers through his hair and plopped his hat back on his head. "The investigator appreciates your offer."

"Who is it?"

"Me. I was a police officer for five years before I became a park ranger. We'll process the crime scene, but something tells me this isn't over."

Drake glanced at the couple's red sedan parked fifty yards away. He'd checked it earlier. "I agree. This is savage, and it doesn't look like anything was stolen from their car."

Taking pictures of the couple and the surrounding terrain and gathering what little evidence there was, Drake worked with Don and another park ranger. When the bodies were transported from the scene, Drake put his gear back in the rear of his SUV. "I'll let you know if the lab finds anything. Whoever did this was careful."

"A pro?" Don asked.

"Probably. I don't think this is a crime of passion. It seems cold and calculated." Hence the lack of evidence. Drake opened his driver-side door. "I need to get back to Cactus Grove. I'll dig into Clarence and Susan's lives and get back to you about the lab report. Let me know what the autopsy reveals." It wasn't unusual for different law enforcement agencies to work together to solve a crime.

"Will do. I'll keep you informed of anything having to do with the case."

As Drake drove out of the park, he pushed his SUV over the speed limit. An urgency gripped him. When his cell reception returned briefly, he noted that Kay had called several times. Something was wrong. He tried calling her hospital room.

No answer.

Then he tried the nurses' station and asked for the head nurse. "I'm sorry. She's tied up right now. Can I help you?"

"Yes, where's the woman in room 236? I called its number, and no one answered."

"I don't know. Maybe having some tests done? Who is this?"

"Texas Ranger Jackson, the man who found the patient."

"Are you coming here?"

"Yes. I'm about an hour away."

"Good. Rosa hopefully should be here, and

you can talk to her. She's been dealing with the patient in 236."

"About what?" Frustration tangled with a foreboding feeling.

"I can't reveal any information over the phone."

Drake gave the woman his cell phone number. "Have Rosa call me as soon as possible."

After he hung up, he put his lights and siren on and floored the accelerator. He entered another dead zone that would last most of the way to Cactus Grove.

When he arrived at the hospital, he quickly parked and hurried into the building. He checked his cell phone. Only a message from the El Paso headquarters was new. Nothing from Kay or the head nurse. The elevator doors swished open on the second floor, and his attention zeroed in on the police officer going into Kay's room.

Heart thumping against his rib cage, Drake quickened his pace, and when he entered 236, he came to an abrupt halt. Her bed was empty, with two police officers standing around it talking.

"Did something happen? Where is Kay?" Drake interrupted.

Officer Emert, whom he'd worked with before, faced Drake. "She's gone. And so is the baby."

THREE

After seeing Kay making her escape on the camera footage of the hallways in the hospital, Drake paced the small security office, wondering what had caused her to flee with the baby. The brief expression he'd glimpsed on her face as she'd sneaked out of her room was one of fear. Had someone frightened her? Had she remembered something about what happened to her? "I need the footage of the second-floor hallway for the few hours before she left."

"Just a sec," the security guard said and punched some keys. "Here it is."

Drake stopped and faced the monitor. When a large man barged into the room without knocking, Drake leaned closer to the screen, counting down how long he remained inside. Rosa and an orderly hurried toward the room. The head nurse paused at the entrance and then entered, leaving the orderly in the corridor. Not long after that, the man left 236 but didn't go far. He slipped inside a storage room a few doors away from Kay. Again, Drake noted the time stamp until the guy reappeared in the hallway and went toward the elevator. What did he do in there for twenty minutes?

The only person who might shed light on the man was Rosa. "Thanks. I need you to send me a photo of the man who came out of the storage room. Also, a picture of Kay leaving her room. Send it here." Drake gave the security guard a card with his cell number and email address. "Keep this footage until I say otherwise."

"Yes, sir."

Drake knew Rosa had left work about an hour ago. Earlier she'd told Officer Emert that she hadn't seen Kay leave with the baby, and from the footage that appeared correct. But she hadn't said anything about that man visiting Kay's room earlier. Maybe the nurse could tell him what she'd seen.

First, Drake stopped at the storage room and went inside. He examined what was really only a large walk-in closet for evidence the guy from the tape might have left behind. Everything appeared in its correct place, so he took latent prints from the inside doorknob, then headed downstairs to the main office to get Rosa's home phone number and address. He was glad she didn't live very far from the hospital.

Soon he pulled up in front of the head nurse's ranch-style house and parked in the driveway. The bright Christmas lights around the front welcomed him as he rang the bell.

A teenage boy opened the door with earbuds stuck in his ears, the sound of a current popular song loud enough for Drake to hear.

"Is your mom home?"

"What?" the kid shouted.

The teen was in his own world. He hadn't even bothered to look at Drake other than a brief glance when he answered the door. Drake pulled out his credentials and waved them in the boy's line of vision. "I need to see Rosa Martinez."

Eyes wide, the adolescent yelled, "Mom, the police are here." He remained in the entrance to the house.

Rosa hurried from the back, waving her hand at her son. "Thanks, Samuel. You still haven't shown me your English paper. It's due tomorrow."

The teen stepped back from the entryway and removed his earbuds, his attention now glued to Drake.

"I need to talk to you about Kay," Drake said to Rosa.

"I'm sorry I had to leave, but I had to pick up Samuel from the school library. I don't know what happened. I went into her room to take

Kaleb back to the children's wing. She and the baby were gone. I notified security, and then an emergency took most of my time after that."

Samuel still hung around, moving slowly toward the hallway.

Kaleb? Had Kay remembered the baby's name? "Can we talk in private?" Drake asked, remembering the times he would do anything to get out of writing a paper for school.

"Sure. The kitchen should be private enough." Rosa sent a glare in her son's direction. He left quickly.

"Is he your only child?"

"Yes, how can you tell?"

"Too quiet here." Drake followed Rosa to the kitchen. "I have a sister near my age who has four children. She lives in Houston. When I visit, the house is always noisy, except when they're all asleep."

"You don't have any children?" Rosa gestured at the table while she walked to the counter and filled a mug. "Do you want some coffee?"

"Sounds good." As Rosa handed him a cup and sat, Drake joined her. "I'm not married. I was once."

"What happened?"

"She was killed in the line of duty. She was a highway patrol officer like I was before I became a Texas Ranger. She stopped a truck driving too fast. The driver shot her."

Rosa took a long drink. "I'm so sorry. Did they catch the killer?"

"Yes, he'd been transporting illegal immigrants." Another reason Drake had wanted to be on the human trafficking task force besides the suspicion about what happened to his younger sister.

"Being a police officer is dangerous. I'm so glad my husband has a boring job reading X-rays. He's a radiologist and should be home from El Paso soon."

As he took several sips, Drake relished the coffee. "I know you talked with the two officers in Kay's room, and they passed on what you told them, but I'm here about an incident that happened a couple of hours before you discovered Kay was gone."

Rosa's forehead puckered. "Incident?" She paused, then said, "Oh, you mean the stranger who came into her room looking for another patient."

"Yes, he was about six feet with dark hair." Drake clicked on the photo the security guard had sent him and showed his cell phone to Rosa.

She nodded. "He was looking for an Amy Grafton. We didn't have a patient on my floor by that name. Later I found there was a patient called that, but on the third floor in room 336—an older woman who was being discharged. He probably wrote down the wrong number."

"You didn't see him after that?"

"No. Why?"

"Because on the security tape, that man left Kay's and went a couple of doors down into a storage closet. He stayed there for twenty minutes, then left."

"That's strange."

"I agree. I'll check with Amy Grafton to see if she knows this man."

"If she doesn't, do you think he took Kay and the baby?"

"Kay left with the child. The man had already disappeared, but something doesn't feel right." Why hide in a storage closet for twenty minutes? Drake sighed. "I won't take up any more of your time. You've put in a long day." He rose.

"Please let me know when you find Kay and Kaleb."

"Did she remember the baby's name?"

Rosa pushed to her feet, tired lines carved into her features. "'Kaleb' came to her, and the child responded to it. It was obvious the baby knew her. But she hadn't recalled anything else. At least that I know of."

Had she recognized the man who entered her room? "If you think of anything else unusual that happened on the floor today, give me a call. You have my card?"

She nodded and walked with him to the foyer. "I'm off for the next two days, but I'll help any way I can. I'll be here."

"Thanks."

Weary, Drake needed sleep after the past two long days, but he still wanted to see if Amy Grafton could help him ID the man in the photo. The police were working on identifying the man. At the moment, he was the only lead Drake had other than the security camera showing Kay leaving the hospital by the back door, dressed in the clothes she'd worn the day before. Then she'd disappeared.

At least she had three hundred dollars. But the money without having ID was strange. Had she been faking not knowing who she was? Was the baby hers? The locket indicated she knew the child somehow. He hoped he would hear soon about the latent prints he took off the inside door handle of the storage closet. He couldn't shake the sense of urgency he felt, as though someone was homing in on Kay and the child—someone she'd been fleeing when he found her?

Kay shrank farther into the shadows of the dimly lit café, the ambience more for couples looking for a night of romance than a woman with a baby. She'd cased the place for an hour before she'd come inside to get off the street and order something to eat. Kaleb was finally asleep, strapped against her chest. The only other place she'd gone after leaving the hospital was a store where she'd used the money she'd found in her jeans pocket to buy necessary items for Kaleb and a clean shirt that didn't look like she'd rolled around in the dirt. She used less than a hundred to equip herself and Kaleb to disappear somewhere in the area until she decided on her next move.

She had no idea who was after her, but deep inside she knew someone was hunting her. She didn't have to remember how she ended up on the canyon floor with a head wound or who she was. That man's appearance earlier sent every alarm bell ringing in her head.

The waitress put the hamburger in front of Kay. "Anything else, miss?"

"Please keep the water glass filled. That's all."

"Be thankful it's not as hot as it was in early fall. I'm looking forward to the holidays and colder days."

What had her previous Christmases been like? As usual when she tried to remember, nothing came to mind.

Kay gave the waitress a smile, then took a bite of the hamburger, thick and juicy. Although she ate as fast as she could because she didn't want to stay too long, she savored the delicious flavors of her meal, especially the onion rings, while trying to figure out where she would sleep tonight. If she got a motel room, her three hundred dollars wouldn't last long. She needed to lie low until she figured out who she was. Maybe she could go to a shelter. Earlier she'd seen one while walking here, across the street from a church.

When she finished her dinner, she relaxed, stroking Kaleb's back. For the past half hour, she'd been able to forget she was totally alone. In the hospital room, she'd contemplated staying and waiting for Drake to return, but as time passed and he hadn't come back, she'd realized she really could only depend on herself. But he was a Texas Ranger. A good guy. Surely she could rely on him to help her.

At the moment, she didn't know whom to believe. *Good men had turned bad.*

Where did that come from?

Did she have firsthand experience with that?

Her head still throbbing, she retrieved a couple of over-the-counter pain relievers and took them with a gulp of water.

The café door opened, and a large party entered, followed by a single man. Nothing about him seemed familiar, but the more people who came into the restaurant, the more she took a risk—why did she feel that way? Overriding every confusing feeling bombarding her, she knew she couldn't sit here any longer. She needed to find a place for the night—even if that meant backtracking into the more populated part of Cactus Grove—and come up with a plan.

She put ten dollars on the table on top of her bill and made her way to the restroom. Inside the family one, she locked the door, laid the blanket on the changing table and put Kaleb on it. He'd been sleeping for the past hour. His eyes slid open, and he began to screw his mouth into a frown.

"I'm here, sweetie." Kay splayed her hand over Kaleb's chest and gently patted him as his eyes closed again. "I won't leave you." As she said those words, she meant every one of them. She didn't need to know officially that Kaleb was her child. Every time she looked at the little boy she saw glimpses of herself in Kaleb's face. Kay's heart swelled with an overwhelming love.

Carefully so Kaleb didn't wake up again, Kay changed the baby's diaper. It was nice being in a room where she didn't have to be constantly vigilant for anyone who could be after her. The café, on the outskirts of town, was getting crowded. She couldn't put off looking for a place to stay any longer.

She strapped Kaleb against her chest, swung

the backpack she'd bought for their belongings over her shoulder, then shoved her hand into her pocket to make sure her money was there. Her fingers grazed a card—the Texas Ranger's.

Call him. He said he would help.

I did, and he didn't call back. Where could he have gone that he'd be out of cell reception that long?

Okay, maybe she hadn't given him that much time to call her back before she left the hospital. But when she'd cracked open the door, peeked into the hallway and seen the stranger who'd come into her room sneaking out of a storage closet, she'd known her decision to leave was the correct one. Something wasn't right. He'd gone to the elevator. She'd used the stairs after she was sure the stranger wouldn't return.

No, she couldn't depend on anyone. Someone close to her had recently said that to her. Who?

She closed her eyes and tried to imagine who it had been. Nothing materialized.

Lord, I need more than a brief glimpse. Help me.

When nothing came to mind, she covered the remaining distance to the door and inched it open. The short hallway was empty. She left the family restroom and crept toward the large room, which held more diners than earlier. All she needed to do was cross the expanse and get outside without drawing attention. She scanned the café, filled with couples and families.

It was now or never. She took a step forward. The main entrance opened, and the stranger from the hospital entered.

Kay froze.

Drake pulled up to his family ranch house, needing to catch some shut-eye, but he didn't think he could sleep. Not when he couldn't find Kay and the baby. Amy Grafton had only confirmed what he suspected. The stranger who had barged into Kay's room didn't have any ties to Mrs. Grafton. So why had the guy been on the second floor? The latent prints he'd taken off the storage closet doorknob had all belonged to people who worked there, except one. It was a partial that didn't match anyone in the database.

Before coming home, he'd gone to his office and grabbed the satellite phone, since there was no cell reception at the ranch—only a land-line—because it was too far out of town. He'd wished he'd thought to do that earlier today— then maybe he would have received Kay's call for help. When he'd worked in Fort Worth, he hadn't had to worry about so many dead zones.

The police were looking for Kay and the baby and would call him if she was found. Even knowing that, he'd driven around the area surrounding the hospital in search of the two for the past hour. He'd be back out there tomorrow morning. In his gut, he felt Kay was in danger. From where—or whom—he didn't know. Between working on the Moore murders and the task force, he knew he needed to find Kay.

He climbed from his black SUV and stood next to it, staring up at the clear sky with stars scattered across the darkness as if they had been tossed haphazardly. The light breeze blew across the flat land, the temperature dropping into the forties.

Would Kay and the baby be warm enough?

Why had she run?

Why hadn't she called him?

"Son, is something wrong?" his father's deep gravelly voice called out.

Drake pivoted toward the front porch. "A long day." He hated bringing his work home. The only reprieve he had from his job was when he came to the ranch at the end of the day.

"Anna saved dinner for you."

Anna Torres had been with the family for years as a housekeeper and cook. She'd often declared taking care of three men was more than a full-time job. "That sounds great. I forgot to eat lunch." Because he'd been driving back to

Big Bend. He'd totally let it slip his mind until his stomach began to rumble about an hour ago.

"She fixed a plate of double portions before going to bed."

Drake mounted the steps to the wraparound porch that faced south and east. "I sure missed her cooking when I lived in Fort Worth. That was one of the reasons I changed to Company E—I was dwindling down to nothing." He'd certainly taken into account being back where he grew up and living with his dad, but the main reason he had taken this assignment was to be part of the human trafficking task force.

Chuckling, his father patted him on the back. "You didn't take long adding a few pounds to your frame."

"I blame that all on Anna." Drake opened the front door and waited for his dad to go first.

In the kitchen, his father pulled a plate out of the refrigerator and stuck it in the microwave to heat up. "I thought you were going to ask the young woman you rescued yesterday to stay here while she recovered."

When they'd spoken last night, Drake had mentioned he might ask her, especially if no one came forward to help her. "I didn't get a chance to ask her. She left the hospital before I returned to her room."

"Why would she do that? Didn't you say she couldn't remember who she was? Did that change?"

Had it, while he was investigating Clarence and Susan's murders? Was that why she was gone? "I don't know, and I don't have a good feeling about this. I think someone is after her and is possibly willing to kill to find her." The more he thought of the couple's murder and the fact a stranger had come into her room, the more he felt Kay was in trouble. When he left her, she hadn't given any indication she would flee. In fact, she'd seemed to appreciate his presence— a familiar face.

The microwave beeped at the same time the back door opened, and his younger brother, Frank, came into the kitchen, plopping his cowboy hat on the peg by the door. "I see you arrived about the same time I finished unloading the hay."

Drake grinned. "Yep, I parked by the gate and waited until you were through. Why do you think I have a pair of high-powered binoculars in my car?"

His brother tossed back his head and laughed. "I always thought because you were a Texas Ranger you needed them for your job, but now I know the truth. Next time I'll keep the barn doors shut so you can't see in."

Drake took his plate out of the microwave and sat at the table. "How's Blue Bonnet?" The mare had been his mother's horse, and ever since their mom died two years ago, Frank had taken extra care of the pinto their mother had loved.

"She fractured her leg and the vet had to set it, but she should heal all right. She has many years ahead of her."

"Sons, I'm heading to bed." Their dad strolled from the kitchen, cradling his mug.

"I didn't even mention Mom." Drake cut his roast beef into smaller pieces.

"I know. He still can't talk about her death. I hope one day when I find the right woman, I have their kind of marriage."

Drake had had that with Shanna—until someone killed her. His family had been there for him when his wife had died five years ago, but no one could erase the pain. He knew what his father was going through. Time had helped, but it couldn't make him forget the devastating loss. "Dad will come around."

"You haven't."

Drake started to reply, but his cell phone rang. Maybe it was news about Kay. He quickly answered the unknown number. "Drake Jackson here."

"This is Kay. I'm in trouble."

FOUR

Kay hunkered down behind a large bush, rocking back and forth to keep Kaleb asleep and quiet. "Someone is after me," she murmured into her throwaway phone.

"Where are you?" Drake asked, the sound of his deep voice calming her frazzled nerves after the harrowing escape through the restaurant kitchen. Had the man from the hospital seen her leave?

She scanned the field behind the café, praying the man wouldn't come out the back door as she had. But when it creaked open, her mouth went dry, and sweat rolled down her forehead.

"Kay, where are you?"

"Behind the Five Star Café," she whispered, but before she could tell him anything else, Kaleb woke up with a jerk, as though he was startled, and began wiggling and whining. "Shh." She leaned over and kissed the top of his head, then stroked his back.

When she looked up, the man had stopped several yards away at the edge of the overgrown field. "I know you're out here. Where are you?"

The taunting menace in his voice struck fear deep into her, and for a few seconds she stopped patting Kaleb. He let out a wail.

Paralysis permeated Kay. Her attention riveted to the man.

He cackled.

She rammed the phone into her pocket, then still in a squat, she pivoted on the balls of her feet, frantically searching for the best direction to escape. With a quick glance over her shoulder, she plunged into the thicker vegetation nearby, whispering to Kaleb, "Shh, sweetie. We need to be quiet."

He continued to fuss but softer, especially when she hunched her shoulder and cradled him even closer to her.

The light from the rear of the café barely penetrated the growing darkness. With another look behind her, though, she clearly saw the large man rushing toward her. She ran through the thicket, branches slapping against her as she increased speed. When she burst out of the undergrowth, a wide stretch of flat land lay before her. Nowhere to hide. She didn't have to glance back to know the assailant was still coming, because the sounds behind her reminded her of a cattle stampede. Dragging in gulps of air, she raced across the field toward the woods.

God, help!

But the man kept coming like a hunter totally focused on its prey. *Pop! Pop!*

He was shooting at her? With a silencer?

A cold determination settled over her. She wouldn't go down without a fight. With every ounce of will, she poured what energy she had into her legs and sprinted faster.

Until she brought her foot down in a hole and went flying forward. She twisted in midair and landed on the hard ground on her side to protect Kaleb.

The sound of the man's pounding footsteps penetrated her dazed mind. She scrambled to rise while Kaleb cried, a beacon alerting her assailant to their location.

The lights of the café beckoned Drake. All he could think about was hearing the baby crying and the fear in Kay's voice right before the line went dead. He clamped the steering wheel even tighter. As he'd rushed out of the house, he'd placed a call to the Cactus Grove police. Although he wasn't that far away from the Five Star Café, he hoped one of their officers could reach her even faster.

Up ahead a patrol car pulled into the parking

lot and headed toward the rear. A minute later, he steered his SUV in the same direction, and when he arrived around back, the sound of gunfire fueled him with urgency. He slammed on his brakes, his vehicle fishtailing and coming to a stop near the patrol cruiser. In seconds, he snatched his night-vision goggles from the front scat, then exited with his weapon drawn.

Drake headed into the field, zooming in on the silhouettes of two men about five yards apart. Another round of shots resonated through the night air as the screech of tires behind him informed him others were joining the foray.

Friend or foe?

Drake quickly threw a look behind him, taking note of more police arriving. With his back covered, he returned his total focus on the two figures in the field. The officer went down, lost in the high weeds, while the assailant pivoted and ran hunched over to the cover of trees farther back from the café. Pursuing Kay? Drake didn't see her.

Still wearing his badge, he gestured toward two patrolmen approaching. "I'm Texas Ranger Jackson. I called this in. There's an officer down. One of you check on him—the other, come with me. I'm going after the shooter, who is pursuing a woman and a baby."

He spun around. *Where are Kay and Kaleb?*

That question drove him after the attacker. Drake signaled for the police officer to search to the left while he covered the right side. When Drake approached the area where the shooter had stood, he inspected the ground for any clue to what happened to Kay. He spied a backpack, grabbed it and slung it over his shoulder, then kept going toward the woods at the rear end of the field, praying Kay and Kaleb were all right.

As he entered the grove, he donned his night-vision goggles. Although the moon was nearly full, the canopy of leaves above him blocked most of its light.

Scanning the terrain around him, Drake penetrated deeper into the trees, his senses heightened. When a deer bounded across his path, he came to a halt, startled. As it raced away, Drake drew in a deep, calming breath and proceeded forward, even more alert.

In the distance, a scream pierced the copse.

The sound of Kay's pursuing assailant consumed her thoughts. She didn't dare slow down as she felt her way through the dark woods, one arm in front with the other clasped around Kaleb. For some reason, he thought she was playing a game and giggled—thankfully not too loud—as her movements jostled him up and down.

The thundering of her heartbeat in her head,

coupled with the pain from her injury yesterday pounding against her skull, vied with her harsh breaths for attention as she dragged air into her lungs. She didn't know how much longer she could keep going. Suddenly she realized she didn't hear her pursuer anymore, but in the distance sirens blared.

Had he given up and fled from the police?

She couldn't keep up her fast pace. She slowed to fortify herself with deeper inhalations and get her bearings. Her arms ached from holding Kaleb for so long. Needing a place to hide, she searched the darkness. Kaleb began fussing, as though he finally sensed the grave danger they were in.

"Shh, sweetie," she whispered and started moving again, not sure which way to go.

A noise to the right startled her. She veered left. The play of light and dark in the woods confused her. Was she still moving away from her assailant? She could no longer tell which direction she was going.

Then a large shadow stepped from behind a tree, and she ran into a solid muscular body.

She immediately knew it was her attacker. His stale-cigarette scent roiled her stomach. He gripped her arms with an ironclad hold. When she yelled for help, Kaleb bawled. Her assailant slapped her, then yanked on Kaleb, but he was secured against her in the baby carrier. The brute cursed and jerked harder.

Kaleb wailed even louder.

As they struggled, Kay kicked the man's shin and pounded his arms. He couldn't take her child. She poured all her energy into protecting Kaleb.

The brute shoved her to the ground, his large bulk hovering above her. She scrambled away. Kaleb's cries filled her ears and motivated her to keep going, backpedaling as fast as she could. She hated that Kaleb was scared.

She glanced at Kaleb—"I'm here"—then covered his ears and screamed for help again.

When she explored the darkness surrounding her, she didn't see her assailant.

Where is he?

"Kay, are y'all okay?" Drake asked behind her.

All the tension in her body siphoned from her. Now she was. "Yes."

Drake clicked on a flashlight and swept the area with the bright beam, then knelt next to her. "He's gone."

A police officer arrived.

"The man's not here." Drake helped Kay to her feet while she tried to calm Kaleb, who was still crying.

Her legs started to give way. She clutched

Drake to keep her balance, and he slipped his arm around her.

"Which way did he go?" the officer asked. "He wounded one of our own."

"I'm not sure. Kay, did you see where?"

"No. It was too dark, and all I could think was to get away from him."

Drake removed his goggles and handed them to the officer. "Use these. It might help."

"Thanks. I've called in more men. We'll have these woods covered in no time. You take care of the lady." The patrol officer headed north.

Drake cradled her against his side. "I'm going to take you back to the hospital, but I won't leave your side."

"No. I won't go there. I'm fine." Or she would be when she and Kaleb were safe.

When will that be?

She didn't know. Nor why someone was after her. *I have to remember how I ended up in Big Bend National Park.*

"Okay. Then I'll take you to my family ranch. My dad was a medic in the army."

"I can't put your family in danger." With her arms wrapped around Kaleb, who had calmed down, she straightened away from Drake. He'd already saved her twice. She couldn't keep depending on him. To emphasize that, she took a couple of steps back in spite of the fact every ounce of her energy was gone.

"Why did you leave the hospital before being discharged?"

"I was scared of that man chasing me." She waved at the place where her attacker had been moments ago. "Earlier he came into my hospital room. Thankfully Rosa quickly answered my call button with an orderly."

"So you know who is after you? Are you remembering what happened to you?"

She peered at Kaleb, wishing she could recall how they ended up in the park. But her memory was a vast sea of nothing. "No…but there was something about the man that scared me."

"C'mon. Let's get you to my car."

With his flashlight shining a path through the woods and field behind the café, Kay began to feel safer—at least for the moment. If the police caught the attacker, then maybe she would get answers to her questions about who she was. Why had she and Kaleb been in the park alone?

One of the Cactus Grove police approached Drake as they neared an SUV behind the café.

Drake paused at the vehicle. "Lieutenant, any sign of the man who attacked this woman?"

"I have everyone I can spare out there looking. So far nothing. It's like he disappeared into thin air."

At hearing the police officer's assessment, Kay slid her eyes closed and leaned back against the SUV. *Please, Lord, give me answers. I feel so lost.*

"How is the downed police officer?"

Drake's question riveted Kay's attention. She'd heard shots behind her as she fled, but she hadn't realized a person was hurt.

The lieutenant glanced at the ambulance leaving. "The paramedics are taking him to the hospital. He was shot in the upper chest, right side. He should make it barring any complications."

"I'm taking Kay and her child to a safe place. Call me if anything changes."

Kay straightened, stroking Kaleb down his back. Safe place? Would she ever be safe? A police officer came to help and was wounded. His presence behind the café allowed her to get away from her assailant, but it had cost the patrolman.

"Will do." The lieutenant shook Drake's hand, then he tipped his hat toward Kay and left.

Drake moved closer as if shielding her. "You don't need to hang out here. Let's go."

"Where?"

"My family ranch. My dad and brother are expecting you and Kaleb."

"But—"

"They would be upset with me if you didn't

come. They won't turn away from someone who needs help."

She searched for the right words to refuse his offer. None came to mind. Already one man had been hurt trying to help her. She had no one but Drake. Kaleb's well-being was her number-one priority. "Okay." She gave Drake a small smile she wasn't sure he saw in the dim light behind the café.

He opened the passenger door and assisted her inside. She followed his progress around the hood of the car, wondering what would have happened to her and Kaleb if he hadn't found her in the park. What if someone like the man from the hospital had discovered her first? The idea of her assailant grabbing Kaleb renewed her fear twofold. Shivers slithered through her, as if a snowstorm had swirled around her.

Drake slipped behind the steering wheel and started the SUV. "The ranch isn't too far from here. That's why I was able to get here so quickly after you called."

"I didn't know what else to do." *I don't know who to trust.*

He threw her a glance, then pulled out into the light traffic. "It looks like Kaleb has fallen asleep."

"He's got the right idea. We've had quite an adventure recently."

"If the guy isn't caught tonight, I have a photo of him from the hospital that I'll send to the lieutenant. With that circulating to every law enforcement agency in the area, I imagine your attacker will either be found soon or have the good sense to flee Cactus Grove."

"I want to know why he came after me."

"So do I. I have something I need to tell you." Pausing for a few seconds, he cleared his throat. "The couple who helped us in the park yesterday was murdered. That's why I left. Their bodies were found in Big Bend. The park ranger called and wanted me to come look at the crime scene."

Murdered? No! "Because they helped me?" She squeezed her hands into tight balls, her fingernails stabbing her palms.

A long moment passed before Drake answered, "I don't know for sure."

"But what do you think?"

"It's possible."

She swiveled toward him. Conscious of Kaleb sleeping against her, she lowered her voice and said, "What are you not telling me?"

He let out a harsh breath. "From the looks of the crime scene, they were—questioned first."

Why? What happened to me to lead to their deaths?

For a few seconds, numbness blanketed her, but it quickly melted away. In its place the nice couple's pain and terror crowded her mind. Tears clogged her throat and stung her eyes. Her chest ached as she drew in shallow breaths. What would that man have done to Kaleb if he'd gotten him away from her? Did he have anything to do with the couple's murders?

As Drake drove through an open gate onto a gravel road, Kay said, "I can't stay with your family. Look what happened to the couple who helped me."

"Clarence and Susan not only helped you but me, too. We have no information to indicate the murders have anything to do with you, though."

"Then why did you tell me?"

"I wanted you to know the reason I wasn't with you earlier in the hospital. And I'm not going to act like it doesn't have anything to do with yesterday, but that's only one of the possibilities."

"What other possibilities are there?"

"Some of my work has taken me to Big Bend and the surrounding area. It could be tied to that. Or the couple came across something they shouldn't have. Maybe they witnessed something that caused them to be murdered."

"I wonder if I could have."

He parked his SUV in a three-car garage attached to a sprawling one-story adobe house. "Have you remembered anything?"

"Not really, other than I feel his name is Kaleb." She looked at the baby, pressed against her content and sleeping, as though he didn't have a care in the world. "I need to remember more, but no matter how much I try, I can't."

The light from the garage illuminated the interior. Drake switched off his vehicle and twisted toward her. His hand clasped the top of her leather seat. "I'm not sure forcing it will make it come faster."

"You're right. It's in God's hands."

"Are you a Christian?"

"Yes," she said without thinking about it.

"Then that's another thing you remember about yourself." A smile lit his eyes and drew her attention to his mouth and a dimple nearby.

"Are you a Christian?"

"If it wasn't for my faith, I don't know if I could keep doing my job."

"Why?"

"I often encounter the worst of humanity."

"Then why do you do it?"

"Because it is what I was called to do."

Listening to him and watching the assurance in his expression, she wanted that—to know what she was supposed to do and be content in her mission. But at the moment, she didn't even know her name.

When the overhead garage light went out, Kay

gasped and sat up straight, scanning the darkness around them.

Drake opened the driver-side door and the dome light brightened the interior. "It goes off automatically after so many minutes unless I flip the switch by the door."

"That's how my garage door works, too." It came out without Kay thinking about what she'd said.

His eyebrows rose. "You remember where you live?"

She tried to picture the place she was talking about, but she couldn't. "I don't know why I said that. I have no idea where I live. In a house? An apartment? Here in Texas or somewhere else?"

"Give it time."

When he exited the car, she kissed the top of Kaleb's head, then pushed open her door. Drake rounded the rear of his SUV, waited until she rose, then leaned in and grabbed her backpack, which he'd found in the field behind the café.

"Don't be surprised if everyone is up to meet you."

"Who's everyone?"

"My father, Tom, and younger brother, Frank, as well as our housekeeper, Anna. She's a second cousin. C'mon. Anna will love having a baby in the house again."

Kay hesitated. Three strangers. She fortified

herself with a deep breath. They were all strangers—except Drake.

At the door into the house, he paused. "For Anna the holidays are the best time of year. She starts with a big Thanksgiving feast and goes nonstop until New Year's."

What had she done for Thanksgiving? That had been last week. Who had she shared it with? Who would she share Christmas with? It seemed a long way off, but it was only three and a half weeks away.

Drake held the door for her while she entered the kitchen first. She came to a halt, facing three unfamiliar people. Kay's heartbeat accelerated.

The older woman with long black hair smiled first and covered the distance to her. "A baby! This will be a special Christmas with the little one here."

Christmas? She couldn't stay that long. She had a life somewhere else—hopefully as far from Texas as possible—and needed to get back to it. Would that be enough to keep her and Kaleb safe? As with everything else, she didn't know. Too many questions. No answers. In her gut, she knew going back to her old life wouldn't be easy even if she remembered.

"Anna, give the lady time to settle in before bombarding her with your plans for the holiday. I'm Tom Jackson, Drake's dad." The older man, with salt-and-pepper hair, stepped forward, holding out his hand for her to shake.

When she did, the strength in his grip reassured her. Drake's father wasn't frail. He conveyed the same sense of self-confidence that Drake had. "Thank you for letting me stay here. It shouldn't be for long. I'm sure I'll remember who I am soon when things settle down."

"What's this fellow's name?" Tom asked.

"Kaleb."

As if he heard his name, Kaleb stirred, blinking his eyes, screwing up his face to cry. But the baby's eyes met hers, and he calmed, wiggling to free himself from the sling.

"Here, let me help you." Drake disconnected the bottom belt that wrapped around her waist.

His touch grazed across her back when he unclipped each shoulder strap with one hand while helping to support Kaleb against her with his other one. As Drake stood behind her and peered at the child, his warm breath bathed her neck and caused goose bumps to streak up her arms.

He'd saved her life tonight—again.

"I made a pallet for Kaleb until the guys can get the playpen from storage and clean it off." Anna skirted around Kay and stood at the door into the hallway. "There's a rocking chair in the bedroom where you'll be staying with your child. I'll show you, Kay, while they go to the barn and bring the playpen back here. That'll keep Kaleb safe in case he wakes up before everyone else."

"That sounds good. This little one needs his diaper changed and a chance to move around. He's been confined to the sling for hours." Kay headed into the corridor, throwing a glance at Drake.

The sear of his gaze held such intensity it robbed her of her next breath. The Lord had picked a good protector for her and Kaleb. It renewed her hope after the harrowing evening evading the man from the hospital.

For a few seconds Kay's fear dominated her expression, but as Drake stared at her in the hallway, slowly a glimmer of light brightened her dark brown eyes. Then she turned away and followed Anna to the guest bedroom.

"I think that's our cue to go get the playpen," his dad said while making his way to the back door.

"I didn't even know we had one anymore." Drake followed his brother out of the house onto the deck.

"Yep, Mom just couldn't get rid of it and the crib after I was born." Frank plopped his hat onto his head. "But our cousin Terri has the crib."

As they walked toward the black barn, his father added, "Your mom knew one day we would need them, and as usual, she was right."

A lump lodged in Drake's throat. The longing in his dad's voice brought forth his own sorrow when his mother and wife died. There wasn't anything he could do to change either death, but he could help Kay, and maybe one day he would have answers concerning his sister's disappearance. It had been a rough fifteen years for the Jacksons, but he'd had a close-knit family to help him. Kay didn't, at least not that she remembered. He'd thought he'd lost her tonight, especially when he heard her scream. But he'd been given a second chance to guard her. He hoped someone had done that for his sister Beth.

His younger brother elbowed his arm. "Drake, quit daydreaming. You said on the phone you would give us the details of what happened tonight?"

Drake looked around the barn, half of the stalls empty, wondering how he'd ended up inside. "Just woolgathering, as Grandpa used to say."

"Thinking about Kay?" His dad swung open the door into the storage area at the back.

"Yeah," Drake said quickly and then launched into an account of what went down behind the café.

By the time Frank and Drake reached the house's back door, lugging the square wooden playpen, Drake had finished with the detailed depiction of what happened to Kay and Kaleb.

His dad whistled. "She's like that she-bear with her two cubs I encountered on a hiking trip. Thankfully she got 'em running away, and she followed rather than charging me. The Lord was looking out for me that day."

After finding Kay, every protective instinct on high alert, in the grove of trees, Drake could agree with his father. She wasn't going to surrender without a fight. "Yep, that's a good description of her, but y'all better not say a word about that to her."

"You two boys go ahead inside. I forgot something in the barn."

After his father disappeared across the yard, Drake exchanged a look with his brother. Their father was going back to say good-night to Blue Bonnet and share his day with the mare, as if he were talking to his wife.

"Let's get moving before the rooster crows." Frank held the playpen and backed into the kitchen while Drake handled the other end.

Drake saw Anna at the stove. "Where's Kay?"

"Rocking Kaleb to sleep."

Drake set his end of the folded playpen down. "Do you want us to put this is the guest bedroom?"

"Only if you're quiet, which will leave Frank

out. Kaleb was fussing when I left. I told Kay I would make a cup of soothing tea for her."

"Who me? Never." One side of Frank's mouth cocked up. His younger brother put his end down, too. "I think I'll also go check on Blue Bonnet before I head for bed."

"Where's Tom?" Anna asked, taking the whistling kettle off the burner.

"He went back to the barn to see Blue Bonnet," Drake said.

"Ah, that's why Frank went back down there. He's worried your dad will never move on."

"What do you think?"

"He will when he's ready. You of all people should know that."

Because he and his father had both lost their wives. He supposed Anna was right. "I'll take this back to the guest bedroom."

"We moved the bed over so you can put it on the left side of it."

He heaved the playpen up and maneuvered his way into the corridor, careful not to bang a wall. He wanted to make things as easy as he could for Kay. When he neared the room, he heard Kay's soft voice singing the words to "Mary, Did You Know." He slowed his steps, not wanting to disturb her, especially since he loved that Christmas song. He set the playpen down against the wall. When her gentle words ended,

Drake remained in place in case she wanted to sing something else.

When she didn't, he peered around the door-jamb. His heart tightened into a fist that seemed to swell in his chest.

Silent tears ran down Kay's cheeks.

Did she remember who she was?

FIVE

While rocking in the guest bedroom chair, Kay cradled Kaleb against her, shutting her eyes to stem the tears running down her face. After she had changed his diaper, the baby still whined, and she'd thought he was hungry. But when Anna fixed a bottle and brought it to her, he didn't want it. The only thing that calmed him was rocking and singing softly. The first song that popped into her mind was "Silent Night," then "Away in a Manger" and finally "Mary, Did You Know." She had no idea where the lyrics had come from, but they had soothed Kaleb.

They'd also calmed her as she'd listened to their message. She couldn't stop the deluge of feelings from all she'd experienced since waking up yesterday—alone and terrified. Both she and Kaleb could have been killed earlier tonight. Why couldn't she remember anything about her past to help identify her? Their lives depended on her recalling. And yet her mind remained blank. She couldn't fall apart. She would find the answers to her problem—for herself and for Kaleb.

When she opened her eyes, her gaze connected with Drake's. He stood in the doorway, his hand clasped around the end of a playpen. The thumping of her heartbeat against her rib cage increased. The kindness in his gaze nearly unraveled the composure she'd fought so hard to retain despite what she was going through.

He smiled and pointed at what he held. She waved him into the room. While his back was to her, she quickly swiped her hand across her face. Had he seen her crying? She didn't want him to worry that she would lose it. She'd dealt with difficult situations and hadn't fallen apart. She wouldn't now, either.

How did she know that? Another tidbit about herself out of the blue, or was it only wishful thinking?

As Drake set the playpen up next to the bed and placed the pallet in it, she shoved away all the questions plaguing her and rose. He stepped away to allow her to lay Kaleb down. For a few seconds, her hand hovered a couple of inches above the baby. When he didn't move or fuss, she straightened, stretching to work the kinks out of her back muscles, then she moved toward the hallway.

Drake followed. "Are you okay? I saw—"

"I was thinking about the words to the songs I sing to Kaleb. They touched me deeply." Hoping he wouldn't ask anything else, she started down the corridor toward the kitchen.

He came up beside her. "They touched me, too. You have a beautiful voice."

"Thank you. I was just glad Kaleb responded to my singing." Kay entered the kitchen and crossed to the kettle on the stove. A mug sat on the counter with a tea bag in it. "Where did Anna go?"

"Back to bed. She's usually the first to go in the evening because she's an early riser—unless I pull an all-nighter. Then I'm up when she gets up."

Kay took a sip of the warm tea, relishing the soothing taste. "I hope I can sleep tonight. I'm exhausted, but I can't right now. Too wired."

"I've gotten so tired before that I can't sleep. Then when I crash, it's hard to wake me up."

She lounged back against the counter. "I hate to ask, but I need a favor."

"I want you to feel you can tell me anything. Ask me anything. I'm here to help."

Kay moved to the kitchen table and sat. When Drake joined her, she finally got up the nerve to say, "I'd like to go back to Big Bend to where you found me."

"That could be risky."

"I know, but I thought it might help me to remember how I got there. Why I was in the park with a baby in the first place. Have the park rangers found any vehicles unaccounted for? Or a backpack?"

"Not that I've heard. They're supposed to let me know if they find something that might be tied to you."

"Either I drove or walked in. What if I had a campsite somewhere? Maybe near where you found me? I didn't have many belongings at the hospital. You don't go hiking, especially with a baby, without certain items—like water. What if someone left me in the park without water, food or hats for Kaleb and me? I can't see me going into it without those supplies and others, especially with a baby." She leaned forward. "Even if I was only going for the day, I would have had more stuff with me."

"Those are all good questions, but with the deaths of Susan and Clarence, I don't think you should go there."

She barely remembered the nice couple, but their murders weighed heavily on her. "Their deaths only emphasize that something very serious is going on. How will I ever be safe if we don't get to the bottom of what's wrong? I have to do what I can to protect Kaleb." As she said the last sentence, she sensed that had been her goal from the very beginning of whatever happened to her. She couldn't shake the sensation, just like she'd known instinctively the man from the hospital was after her, and that had turned out to be true.

Lines creased Drake's forehead. "Let me investigate. That's my job."

"If I had good information on what was going on, I'd let you handle everything. But my memory loss is impeding the investigation. I *must* remember who I am. The park may be the key."

"What about Kaleb? Are you going to leave him while we go?"

Now it was her turn to frown. She hadn't thought beyond revisiting the place where Drake had found her. Should she leave Kaleb at the ranch? Could she? "I can't take him back to the park. I'd leave him with the right caregiver if he was safe. Until tonight at the café, I'd been hoping I was overreacting to that man showing up in my hospital room. But now I know I wasn't. Maybe if he's caught we can go or…" She shrugged. "I don't know what to do. That's the problem."

Drake covered her clasped hands on the table. "How about this. Give it a day or two to see if your attacker is tracked down. The police are splashing his photo all over the media in the area. The guy not only came after you and Kaleb, but he injured one of their own."

The feel of his touch reinforced she had someone to help her. She smiled. "Thank you. I don't know what I would have done without you. I should have kept calling until I got hold of you earlier instead of panicking."

Returning her grin, a light shining in his blue eyes, Drake squeezed her hand, then slipped his away. "You need rest. Don't worry tonight. My brother and I are taking turns staying up and guarding the house. Frank was in the Marines for four years and part of a security detail."

"I hate that you and your brother are losing—"

"Don't worry about us. We'll be fine. I'll sleep better knowing Frank is watching out for us, and he will when I get up. We aren't the ones recovering from an injury."

Kay sighed, massaging her left temple as if that would erase the throbbing ache pulsating in her head. "Yes, and my body is reminding me of that right now."

"Tomorrow you should talk to your doctor to make sure you're doing everything you need to do. How about Kaleb?"

"He was being released, but I'll ask about him as well as talk with the state case worker." She rose, took the mug to the sink and rinsed it out.

Drake opened the dishwasher and put it inside. "Let me talk with Kaleb's case worker first."

"Maybe…" Suddenly she didn't want to voice her thoughts out loud.

"What?"

"Tonight I got the feeling my attacker wanted Kaleb. The baby was strapped to me, and the man was furious when he couldn't get Kaleb away from me. What if I'm not his mother?"

"There's one way to prove that. I can do a DNA test. It'll take a while to get results, so in the meantime, we'll continue to investigate who you are and offer you both protection. There has been no Amber Alert put out on Kaleb, and the locket shows you have a connection to him. I'll stress that with the authorities."

But why was I in Big Bend? "Let's do the DNA test. That'll solve one problem." She started for the hallway, trying to stifle a yawn, but she couldn't. "I think that's my cue to say good-night."

"We'll talk more tomorrow. Oh, and by the way, in the evening we'll be decorating our Christmas tree. We've always done it at the beginning of December. You and Kaleb are welcome to participate."

Maybe being involved would help her remember what she used to do in the past at Christmastime. "I'd like that." Kay stood for a second in the kitchen doorway, then strolled in the direction of the guest bedroom, part of her not ready to go to bed. Sleeping left her vulnerable.

After getting ready for bed, she stood over the playpen watching Kaleb. The feeling that she'd watched him sleep before inundated her. The sense she was fighting an unknown enemy in a pitch-dark world wouldn't let go. When she sank down on the mattress, her gaze still glued on the baby, she bowed her head and prayed for answers to her questions.

She finally switched off the lamp on the nightstand, glad Anna had added a night-light in case she needed it. The soft glow comforted her. She could still make out Kaleb in the playpen. She released a long breath and lay down. Sleep descended quickly...

The blackness crept toward her like an insidious fog devouring everything in its way. A man, his face shrouded in shadows, emerged from the mist. His long strides lengthened even more, and suddenly his large bulk was all she saw, but his features were still hidden. He murmured something in Spanish, then with lightning speed his hands locked around her throat.

Squeezing.

Choking off the air.

The lack of oxygen scorched her lungs. Her vision went in and out of focus until...

Kay's eyes bolted open, sweat dripping off her face. She stared up in the dimness at a white ceiling.

Certain she had been strangled, she touched her neck. Quickly she pushed back the covers, looked to make sure Kaleb was still sleeping, then hurried into the bathroom connected to the bedroom. Before looking at herself in the mirror, Kay braced herself for what she would see.

Late afternoon the next day, Drake entered the den where his family always set up their Christmas tree in front of a window that showcased it from the front lawn. Kay glanced at him, then returned her attention to Kaleb, who was trying to gum a wooden ornament.

Ever since Drake had seen her this morning and taken a DNA sample, an emotional distance had seemed to grow between them. Something wasn't right. She hadn't said a word to him about going back to Big Bend. In fact, she'd been quiet through the morning and afternoon. Had she remembered what happened to her? They hadn't been able to talk because of all the time he'd been on the phone to his office, the state case worker and the police. Plus, Kay had been dealing with Kaleb and helping Anna as much as possible, but he would find time to talk to her before the day was over. Any loud sound made

Kay nervous and uptight. He couldn't blame her, but he wanted to reassure her the police were closing in on her attacker.

He wove his way through the boxes of Christmas decorations and eased down beside her on the couch. Kaleb sat with Kay, watching his dad and Frank put the lights on the tree while fighting his need to take a nap.

"He still hasn't gone down?" Drake asked, clasping Kaleb under his arms and swinging him to his lap.

"No, and I should probably try to keep him up now and put him down early tonight."

"With all the changes he's had lately, he's likely confused. His sleep pattern is all messed up."

"Especially since I don't remember his usual schedule. No telling how far off we are."

Drake leaned close to her and murmured, "What's bothering you?"

"Lack of sleep."

"Didn't you get about ten hours last night?"

"No, I had a nightmare and was up a few hours before I could go back to sleep."

"What kind of nightmare?"

"A bad one." Kay twisted toward him, staring at Kaleb for a moment, then saying in a whisper, "Someone was strangling me. I couldn't tell who, but it felt real to the point that I got up and went into the bathroom to check for marks around my throat. I couldn't stop shaking. But there was no evidence it was real. I've never had a dream be so realistic. I was sure I would see red marks around my neck, but I didn't."

"Can you describe the person attacking you? Was it the man from the hospital?"

"I couldn't tell much of anything other than the person was large and strong. I guess it could be the guy from the hospital, but for some reason I don't think so." She shrugged. "Maybe I'm letting all this get to me. I need to chalk it up to a nightmare and let it go."

Drake wasn't so sure. Dreams could be a way of letting the subconscious come forward. What if her suppressed memories were driving what happened last night? What if someone had tried strangling her, and that was what caused her to flee with Kaleb? "Let me know if you dream it again."

She arched one eyebrow. "You think there's some truth in my nightmare?"

"It's possible. But if someone left bruises on your neck, it would have been a while ago, because you don't have any now."

"You might be right." Kay crossed her arms over her chest, a shudder rippling through her.

Kaleb turned and leaned toward Kay with his hands opening and closing.

"I think this fella wants his mama." Drake lifted the baby off his lap and settled him in her embrace.

Kaleb rubbed his eyes and whimpered as he tried to get comfortable against Kay.

"This must be my cue to rock him to sleep. I'm glad I fed him a while ago. He might even sleep through the night." Kay scooted to the edge of the couch, then pushed herself to a standing position while trying to keep Kaleb from wiggling out of her arms.

She wobbled, and Drake hurriedly steadied her, leaning partially against her. His heartbeat kicked up a notch at her nearness, and for a few seconds he relished the touch.

Then he remembered where they were and her situation. He quickly lowered his arms and sidestepped away from her. For a moment, he'd forgotten that he'd lost his soul mate. The pain of Shanna's death had nearly done him in. He wouldn't open himself up to being hurt like that again. One love of his life was all he needed.

While Frank and his dad finished stringing the lights, Drake took the opportunity to go outside and case the area. Although it wasn't common knowledge that Kay had come home with him last night, he wasn't going to take any chances. In two days, there had been two murders and an officer wounded. He had to remember Kay was a victim in need, and that was all. He would protect her as best he could. He hoped he could get her home before Christmas. Then he could go on with the life he'd mapped out for himself. But not before she and Kaleb were safe.

A chill hung in the air. Its coldness nipped at his arms. He hurried his pace as he circled the ranch house shaped like a boxy U. As he rounded the west side of his home, he spied a black truck passing the front gate, probably only going twenty miles per hour. He stopped and ducked behind a clump of deer grass at the corner. The pickup slowed to a crawl near the entrance to the property, and instinctively Drake put his hand where his gun was. Then suddenly the driver accelerated and continued down the two-lane highway.

The incident only reinforced his need to be extra vigilant, even at the family ranch, where he'd always felt safe. He couldn't let his guard down, no matter where he was, nor could he do this alone and still investigate Kay's case.

He withdrew his cell phone and called Dallas Sanders, another Texas Ranger in the area. When he didn't answer, Drake left a voice mail, then backtracked and entered the house through the kitchen door.

The scent of hot chocolate infused the room. Since he could remember, they'd always drunk it while decorating the Christmas tree. First his mother had made it, and now Anna did, even if the temperature outside was in the seventies or above. As he crossed to the stove to fill the mugs on the counter, Kay came into the kitchen.

"Did Kaleb go to sleep?" he asked as he poured the hot chocolate.

"I didn't even have to rock him."

"Considering all that has been going on, he's a trouper."

Kay stopped next to him. "I'll help you take these into the other room. The smell is what drew me here. That and the peppermint candles on the mantel are getting me into the Christmas mood."

"The hot chocolate and peppermint are two traditions we do every year."

"I wish I could remember what traditions I followed at Christmastime."

He'd always taken for granted what they did every year at this time. But seeing Kay's melancholy made him realize following traditions each year was comforting, a reminder that some things stayed the same even in a rapidly changing world. "This will be Kaleb's first one. You can start your own."

"I don't even know where I'm going to be in three weeks. How can I—"

He held up his index finger to his lips. "Shh.

We'll take it one day at a time. You've been re-calling a few details. And you're welcome to stay here until you know what to do."

"I appreciate that, but I won't overstay my welcome. You're right. I'll probably remember in no time." She snapped her fingers, then took two mugs and started for the hallway.

Drake managed the other three cups and fol-lowed, the sound of Christmas music drifting to him. "I have to warn you. From now until the twenty-fifth, that will be all you hear around here. Anna would play it year-round if Dad let her."

"That's another reason I like Anna. The music is uplifting, and right now I can use that."

Drake paused at the entrance to the den, watching Kay cover the distance to Anna and give her a mug. Something his cousin said caused Kay to laugh. For a few seconds, her whole face lit up.

"It's about time you brought the hot choco-late, bro. Putting up lights is hard work." Frank grasped his mug while Drake handed one to his father. "Now it's your turn to work." His younger brother sat on the couch and gestured toward the decorations. "As I understand it, no one is ex-empt from putting up ornaments."

Drake settled on the other end of the sofa and sipped his hot chocolate. "Anna, this is delicious."

"A warning, Kay. These two like to argue about who does the most work. Frank, it seems Drake is the one who got the tree and set it up in here."

Frank snorted.

Drake laughed. "Kay, this too is a tradition every year I'm home."

She took a drink, then set her mug on a coaster on the coffee table. "Well, you two can lounge all you want. I'm going to start. It'll be nice to do something like this."

"And I'll help you." Anna rose, followed by all three men.

By the time they finished, the top half of the tree had been filled in by the guys while the bottom was left to Kay and Anna. Drake stepped back, admiring the women's carefully placed decorations—the upper part looked like a demolition team had swept through. He chuckled. That happened every year.

Kay and Anna talked as though they had known each other for years. Drake sighed. He couldn't even begin to imagine what it would feel like not to remember who you were or where you lived.

At that moment Kay, on the other side of the tree, looked at him. She smiled and gave him a nod, and all of a sudden, he and Kay were the only two people in the den. He heard his family speaking, but nothing else mattered except the link of his gaze with hers.

Kay's eyes bolted open for the second night in a row. Sweat drenched her. Her gaze drilled into the ceiling above her. The sensation of being strangled overrode every other awareness. Her harsh exhalation reverberated through the silence. Her throat burned as though hands were still around her neck, squeezing the life from her. At least this time she didn't feel like she'd really been throttled.

When she finally rolled her head toward the nightstand, the red numbers on the clock indicated she'd slept at least five hours, although it seemed like she'd gone to bed less than thirty minutes ago. She pushed up to a sitting position and checked Kaleb in the playpen. Relieved he was still sleeping, she scooted to the edge and rose. She took a fresh change of clothes and dressed in the guest bathroom. Before she left, she again checked her neck for red marks or bruises. Nothing, but it hadn't felt like nothing.

Then she quietly left the bedroom and headed down the hallway in search of Drake. At this time, he would be on guard, and she didn't want to be alone. She checked the kitchen first, then spied a light from the living room. She stopped at its entrance. Empty.

Where is he?

The silence and dimness of her surroundings unnerved her. Her hands shook, and she stuffed them into her jeans pockets. Maybe this wasn't a good idea. She should have stayed in her bedroom and turned to go back there.

Drake came out of the den at the other end of the corridor. When he saw her, he smiled and started for her. "Trouble sleeping?"

She nodded while she shoved down her anxiety. She hadn't wanted to go back to her bedroom—to her nightmare.

He clasped her upper arm. "Is it the dream again?"

"Yes."

"I was going to the kitchen to get more coffee. Want some?"

"Sounds good."

After he filled two mugs and gave one to her, he said, "Let's go into the den and admire our stunning work on the Christmas tree."

Kay followed him, and when she glimpsed the lit up eight-foot-tall tree across the room, emotions from sadness to delight swamped her. For a second, an image of herself placing a glittering star on a small white pine—no more than five feet tall—flashed into her thoughts, only to flee as fast as it appeared. She sucked in a deep breath and stepped back, her hand wobbling so much her coffee sloshed onto her skin.

Drake quickly took her mug and set hers and his on an end table. "What's wrong?"

"I just had a memory of when I was a little girl—at least I think I did."

"Tell me about it." He closed the space between them.

His nearness calmed the trembling, reassuring her she wasn't alone dealing with whatever was going on with her. She described the image she'd glimpsed. "It was like I was watching myself put the star on a partially decorated tree. There was a vague picture of a woman behind me. She might be my mother, but I didn't see her face well. Or it was wishful thinking. I don't—" her voice caught, and she swallowed several times "—know. Even so, how is that memory going to help me, or for that matter, the nightmare I've been having?"

He grasped her hand and held it between them. "Maybe not the one about your past specifically, but it means you're starting to recall childhood memories. That's good news."

"My nightmare lasted a little longer tonight. I saw a huge gold ring on the man's right hand. I tried to see what was carved on it, but I woke up before I could make it out."

"What did it look like? Did it have stones in it? All gold?"

"All gold with something like—a crest on the flat surface. If it was a family crest, that might help."

"Possibly."

She squeezed her eyes closed, rubbing her fingertips against her temple, and tried to picture the ring. Frustration churned her stomach. "I can't remember what the crest looked like."

He clasped both shoulders. "Don't force it. Relax." His strong fingers kneaded her tight muscles.

But the tension clung to her like a second skin. How could she relax with all that was happening to her and Kaleb? There was an unknown enemy out there with unsavory intentions. She shrugged from beneath his hands and moved back. "Now more than ever, I need to go back to Big Bend. If my memory can recall a few facts here, think what could happen if we returned to where it all began."

"Okay, but give me a day to make sure we have enough protection for Kaleb. I don't like the fact your attacker is running around—" His cell phone rang and interrupted him. He quickly withdrew it and looked at the screen. "I've got to take this. It's the police station."

SIX

A few hours later, Drake opened the front door to allow Texas Ranger Dallas Sanders into his family home. "I'm glad you could come on such short notice. We're having breakfast. I hope you brought your appetite."

Dallas took a deep breath. "Ah. Bacon, biscuits and coffee. I never turn down a home-cooked meal, especially since my cooking skills are sorely lacking."

"Come into the kitchen, and I'll introduce you to everyone." Drake walked down the hallway toward the back of the house.

"I'm glad the guy who attacked Kay was caught early this morning. Maybe he'll have answers that will help her remember who she is."

Before going into the kitchen, Drake stopped a few feet from the entrance and lowered his voice. "You're staying here while we go to the police station, then the national park is just a precaution. If we get all the answers when the man's interrogated, I'll let you know, and then you can leave if you want. Maybe you'll be able to make your daughter's music program in time this evening. I hate taking you away from family."

"Hold it right there. Michelle understands." Dallas grinned. "I'll get my own private music show later tonight. I'm continuously surprised by her musical talent. She didn't get it from me."

Drake had hoped to be a dad by now. Shanna and he had wanted a family but had been waiting, so when his wife's autopsy came back, showing she'd been eight weeks pregnant, he'd been stunned. He wasn't even sure Shanna knew she'd been expecting. He'd kept that news quiet, private, and he was usually okay except for the moments he held Kaleb or others talked about their children. Then the what-ifs would fill his thoughts.

As he continued into the kitchen, his gaze immediately went to Kay, then Kaleb. He'd missed being a father, but perhaps it was for the best. His job was too risky.

Drake introduced Dallas to his family and Kay. After his associate sat, Drake took his chair next to Kay. "We need to leave in a few minutes. Captain Vincent wants you to ID the man who attacked you in a lineup, then he'll interview him."

"Are we staying for that?" Kay scraped the

last bite of a smashed banana into a spoon, then fed it to Kaleb, who eagerly ate it. "He definitely likes bananas."

On the other side of the high chair—another piece of furniture that had been in storage—Anna picked up the bowl of oatmeal. "Finish your breakfast, Kay. I'll take care of the little man."

Kay's forehead creased. "Are you sure about watching him?"

"Yes, I've wanted to dote on him since y'all came. It'll give me an excuse not to work today."

Kay laughed. "I have a feeling you'll work harder than usual."

"I have a niece and nephew. I know what I'm getting into," Anna said with a chuckle.

Drake still wasn't convinced going back to the park was a good idea. He remembered the sight of the murdered couple. But if it helped Kay recall who she was, then he guessed it was worth the risk.

By eight in the morning, Drake stood by his SUV in the garage while Kay kissed Kaleb, then relinquished him to Anna. Dallas stood behind them watching, while Frank and their dad had gone to the barn to do the necessary chores.

As Kay hurried toward him, her eyes glistened with unshed tears. She hadn't insisted on going to the park without weighing the pros and cons. He could imagine the fear and hesitation she was experiencing. She needed her memory back to move forward, but that meant taking a big risk. He'd do what he could to keep her safe. Besides the people in this house, no one else knew they were going to Big Bend. After what happened at the hospital, he made sure he had a satellite phone in case something came up and they needed help. But even a sat phone didn't always work. It would depend on the weather and terrain.

"Okay?" Drake opened the passenger door for her.

"I will be, especially if I find answers today." Kay slid into the front seat.

When Drake started the car and backed out of the garage, he threw her a glance. "I'm thinking positive. At least the guy after you is in jail." He hoped that was who the police had caught. They'd had a good photo of him to go by, but he'd breathe easier after Kay identified her attacker. He also hoped when he went to the park, he could tell Don Calhoun the Moores' killer was in jail. The man who was arrested had been driving a newer car, so the police were using its GPS to track his whereabouts. Drake would know when he got to the station if Kay's assailant had been in Big Bend in the past week.

"And we might even get answers to who I am from him. Are they running his fingerprints?"

"Yes, although his prints don't match anyone in the database so far. But that was also true of a set I took from the hospital storage closet. The guy they have in custody matched those prints. They're expanding the search internationally, since we're so close to the border." Drake pulled onto the highway and drove toward Cactus Grove.

"Why me? I can't stop asking myself that."

"Let's hope he'll tell us." Many criminals would confess for a lighter sentence, or they would trip themselves up while being interrogated. He hoped that was the case with this suspect.

"Has anyone turned in a missing-person report on someone like me?"

"No, but the search has expanded to the Southwest United States. We're also asking quietly about a missing baby around Kaleb's age. I've called in a favor, and we should have the DNA paternity test results back in a few days. Before the attack, I would have advised using the media to see if we could find out who you are, but with the assault, I hesitate to do that." A missing baby was usually big news, with an Amber Alert sent out to all law enforcement agencies. If Kaleb was

Kay's baby, then that could explain why there hadn't been one.

"Thanks. What if the guy who came after me was hired by someone else? I can't shake that feeling."

Drake stopped at a light and twisted toward Kay. Fear shadowed her eyes, her mouth turned down in a frown. "That's why Dallas is at the ranch as an extra precaution. Too many unknowns with this case."

Kay remained silent the rest of the way to the police station. Her body screamed tension, from her hands twisting together in her lap to her ramrod posture. There was nothing else he could say to ease her concerns. He hoped the interrogation would provide answers.

Kay stood behind a two-way mirror as the lineup of men filed into the room. The second her assailant entered, a cold, clammy feeling washed over her. The man had played tug-of-war with her, using Kaleb. She would never forget his rough features, framed by the light over the back door of the café as he scanned for her location.

She waited until the six men stopped and faced her before saying, "He's number two."

"Are you sure?" the captain asked.

"Yes, definitely."

"Good. Then we'll interview him next." Captain Vincent looked at Drake. "Do you want to be in on it?"

"No, I'd like to observe with Kay. She's hoping something he says will trigger a memory."

As the captain left, a police officer escorted her assailant into the interview room. Kay stepped back from the two-way mirror. The man's gaze bored into the glass, as though he could reach across the space separating them and grab her. The sensation of his hands gripping her arms as they had the other night flooded her senses—the rancid odor of cigarettes and sweat, the tight pressure of his grasp, the looming image of his large bulk. For a few seconds, she was transported to the woods behind the café, fighting to keep Kaleb.

"Kay?" Drake clasped her hand and gave it a gentle squeeze. "He can't hurt you now."

She closed her eyes, relishing the feel of his grasp, Drake's warm palm against her cold one. "I'm recalling that night in the woods."

"Give it time."

"Why do I feel I don't have time?"

"I don't know, but you aren't alone now. We'll figure it out."

Finally, she slid a glance in his direction, taking in the caring in his blue eyes, the intensity pouring off him, the determination in his facade. She twisted toward him, cupping his hand between hers. The tangible and intangible connections that linked them drove the fear away.

She smiled. "Thanks for being here."

Captain Vincent joined her assailant in the interview room and sat next to him. "You were identified as the man who attacked a woman in the field behind the Five Star Café and wounded a police officer. Those are serious crimes. My officer is still in the hospital, so let's start with an easy question. What is your name?"

The pockmarked man snorted and pressed his lips tightly together.

"If you think not telling us who you are will stop you from being prosecuted, think again. It won't. We're running your fingerprints."

Her attacker smirked.

"Both here and overseas, starting with Mexico, since we're so close to that border. Your photo will be sent, too."

The cocky grin disappeared.

"Someone is bound to know you. I'm sure this isn't your first time breaking the law."

"I want an attorney," the man said in Spanish.

And Kay understood what he'd said. She knew Spanish, which became evident when the captain replied in that language. Another tidbit about herself, but she needed so much more.

"I know what they're saying. Do you think

he's from Mexico? Maybe that's why you haven't been able to match his fingerprints."

"His prints were sent there this morning," Drake replied.

Finally, Captain Vincent rose. "You'll make a call to your lawyer, then be taken back to a cell until he arrives."

"Let's go." Drake started for the door. "We have a long day in front of us." Out in the hallway, he approached the captain. "We need to leave for Big Bend. Even with a sat phone, reception can be spotty, depending on weather and location. I'll try calling you when I can pick up reception to see if you get anything from him."

"Don't worry. This guy isn't going anywhere. Besides Kay's ID of him, we have his gun, and it's a match to the one used in the shooting of our officer."

"Any useful information from the GPS in his car?"

"Yes. He was in Big Bend the time you were concerned about."

Which meant he could have killed the couple who'd helped her—maybe he'd been trying to get information about Kay from them. He most likely had been tracking her.

After Drake shook hands with his childhood friend, Captain Vincent, he escorted Kay from the building, his gaze sweeping the area as they walked to his SUV. "You okay?"

She nodded.

"Did you get any impressions from the suspect?"

"Other than the fact that I know Spanish, no more than what I already felt—a sense I've seen him before he came to my hospital room. What if I saw him in Big Bend?"

"That's possible." Drake stopped at the passenger door and opened it for her. "Could he be Kaleb's father?"

She shuddered. "No!"

"How can you be sure?"

"I just am. When the DNA test comes back, you can compare his with the results."

"I don't think he is, but I had to ask."

Kay climbed into the vehicle as another tremor shook her. She couldn't explain how she knew the suspect wasn't Kaleb's father, but he wasn't. Maybe it was because the first time she saw him, he didn't have any kind of reaction to her holding Kaleb. There was nothing in his expression except coldness.

As Drake pulled out of the parking lot, Kay visualized her son as she last saw him—trying to grab the spoon Anna had been using to feed him, giggling as though he were playing a game.

"Can I use your phone to call Anna and see how Kaleb is doing?"

"Sure."

Kay picked up the sat phone and made the call. The need to connect with him overwhelmed her as though this could be the last time. When Anna answered, Kay suddenly didn't want to go to the park. The impulse to have Drake turn around inundated her, but the words wouldn't come out. Answers lay in Big Bend.

"How's Kaleb doing?" Kay asked.

"He's playing with the stacking rings Frank bought him while in town this morning. I think he's teething. I'll hold the phone up to his ear."

Kay waited until Anna indicated Kaleb was listening. "It's Mama, Kaleb."

Her son rattled off a string of nonsense words, but again he said, "Mama."

The sound lifted her spirits. "I hope you're having fun with Anna. I'll be back soon. I love you, Kaleb." And she meant that last sentence more than anything.

"Everything all right at the ranch?" Drake asked when she hung up.

"Yes, Frank bought a toy for Kaleb." She wanted to be in two places at once—or she wished Kaleb was here with her. But the ranch was the safest place for him right now. She didn't have anything to worry about with her attacker at the police station and Dallas Sanders at the ranch as a precaution.

"It'll be a couple of hours. I know you haven't gotten a lot of sleep lately. Why don't you take a nap while I drive?"

"I can say the same about you. I'm sure I know how to drive if you want to get some rest."

He shot her an amused look. "I'm a law enforcement officer. You don't have a driver's license on you. We'll leave it as is."

"Well, then that leaves us getting to know each other. Or rather, me getting to know you, since I don't remember anything about my past I haven't already told you. There's a family photo in the living room. I recognized your dad. Was the woman next to him your mother?"

"Yes."

"So you have three siblings. Frank lives at the ranch. Where are your sisters?"

Drake didn't reply. He clenched his jaw, and his knuckles whitened as he held the steering wheel.

"Did I say something wrong?"

"I only know where one of my sisters is. Mandy lives in Houston with her husband and four children." He paused for a long moment, the stress in the vehicle skyrocketing. "My other sister—"

"You don't have to tell me unless you want to," Kay quickly said, hearing the pain in his voice.

Again, a long silence, as if he was wrestling with himself about what he should do.

Kay leaned toward him and touched his arm. "I shouldn't have asked. Forget the question." She didn't want to bring any sorrow to this man who'd been there for her.

"No, maybe I should talk about it more. Keeping things locked up inside hasn't helped. What happened to Beth is the reason I went into law enforcement. I was a senior in college when she came to Dallas to go to the same university I did. That year I met my future wife, and we were getting serious. I should have been watching out for Beth more. She disappeared from campus. There was a massive search for her, but she'd vanished. Later, a human trafficking ring was discovered in the area, and evidence pointed to my sister being abducted. Beth wasn't the only college student who went missing that year."

"I'm so sorry to hear that, Drake. It's hard enough losing a sibling, but to have one disappear and not know where she is must be twice as bad."

He cleared his throat. "I should have been there for her more. Kept a better eye on her."

"Short of locking her up or following her around 24-7, you couldn't have prevented what happened."

The terrifying image of being strangled

flooded Kay's mind. Burning lungs. Pain as she struggled to breathe. She heard a snap, and her head fell forward as though the man had snapped her neck. Kay cupped her throat. Sweat broke out on her face.

"Kay, what's wrong?"

"I—I…" The picture vanished as fast as it had appeared. Was she going to be haunted by her nightmare even when she was wide awake?

God, help me. What's going on?

"Kay!"

The sound of Drake's voice dragged her back to the present. When Kay focused on her surroundings, she found the car parked on the side of the highway. She hadn't even realized he'd pulled off the road. Was she going mad?

"Kay, what just happened? You're pale. You're shaking."

She folded her arms over her chest and glanced at him. "I had my nightmare wide-awake. But this time, he killed me. He snapped my neck. I was there. I felt it."

Drake leaned close, his arm sliding along her shoulders. "Did you see who was strangling you?"

"No. It happened so fast, all I thought about was trying to stay alive." She shifted to face him. "I'm alive. Why am I dreaming this? I feel like I'm going crazy. What is my mind trying to tell me?"

"I don't know. Something bad must have happened that possibly led to you being in Big Bend. Or it might—" he kneaded the tight muscles in her neck "—have nothing to do with you personally but someone else."

"I witnessed a murder?"

"Maybe."

"Then it's even more important that we go to the park."

"I agree. Someone could have been murdered. It wouldn't be that hard to dispose of a body and it not be found. There's a lot of rugged, desolate places in the park."

Kay peered out the windshield at a bank of clouds building up in the direction of Big Bend. "Then we'd better get going. I want answers. I want this to end today."

"It might not, Kay. You might walk away with more questions."

"Then I'll deal with that when it happens. I want my life back." She hated the sound of desperation that leaked into her voice, but it wasn't only about her. Kaleb was involved, too. He depended on her.

As Drake approached the place where he'd originally found Kay, he glanced at the sky, the cloud cover growing. He wasn't sure how well his sat phone would work with the canyon walls and the clouds. Earlier, he'd called Park Ranger Don Calhoun and told him that he was returning with Kay to where she'd been injured. He hadn't wanted to stop at the visitors' center. The fewer people who knew they were here, the better they would be, especially when he remembered the murdered couple. They'd talked a few minutes about the Moore case, but whoever had committed the murders had covered his tracks well. The gun the guy arrested in Cactus Grove had used to shoot the police officer hadn't matched the one used to kill Clarence and Susan.

"This is the place." He indicated the rocky ground, and the spot where Kay's head wound had bled into the dirt was still faintly evident. "I'm not sure why you were here. The large boulder at that time of day protected you from the sun and concealed you if you'd been hiding from someone. Does any of this seem familiar?"

Her brow wrinkled, she slowly rotated in a full circle. "You think that was why I was behind the boulder?"

"Even if no one was after you, you'd have wanted to stay in the shade as much as possible. You didn't have a hat on, and you weren't carrying water."

She examined the ground where she'd lain.

"This is uneven, not easy to walk over. I could have fallen. Where was Kaleb in relationship to me?"

"A foot away. Here." Drake pointed to the place that was relatively even and without rocks. "If you fell, Kaleb most likely wasn't in your arms."

"What if someone was after me and I hid behind here? Maybe I put Kaleb down, then went to the boulder and peeked around it to see if anyone followed us? I could have fallen coming or going."

"That's a possibility." He waved his arm toward a large stone slab. "Let's sit and eat the lunch Anna made for us. Maybe something will come to you."

"I hope so." While Drake grabbed his backpack, Kay eased down on the rocky perch. "I hate being away from Kaleb for nothing. All this must be confusing for him. It certainly is for me. Thankfully kids don't remember what happens to them at his age."

He sat next to her and passed her a wrapped sandwich. "It's a turkey salad sandwich. I hope you're not tired of turkey by now. That's mainly what we've had since Thanksgiving. Anna gets the biggest one, so we have lots of leftovers."

"I don't remember Thanksgiving." Kay took a bite of her sandwich and chewed it slowly. "But

I love turkey and even prepare it at other times during the year." The second she said the last sentence, she tilted her head toward him, her eyes huge. "I've done it again. A memory coming to me out of the blue."

"Taste and smell can stir memories. Do you remember anything else? Who you were with? Where you were?"

She stared at the ground in front of her while she ate another bite. "Not much. But I think the landscape around here reminds me of where I live."

"That excludes a lot of places, but the southwestern part of the United States is a large area."

"Maybe it's only about where I grew up."

"Give it time." Drake passed her a bottle of water, then started eating his lunch.

Silence fell between them. He didn't want to push her, but he didn't have much to go on. He'd hoped the assailant in jail would talk. He still might after visiting with his lawyer. If the man's fingerprint identification came through, then at least Drake would have a lead he could follow. So far, all the others had led to dead ends.

"What do we do now?" Kay asked as she wadded up her trash and passed it to him to put in the backpack.

"I'd like to explore this canyon. If you had a

campsite, it might be in here farther back. Ready to go?"

"Yes. I feel better when I'm doing something to find answers." Kay hopped off the stone ledge and faced him. "What if my memory never returns completely?"

"You'll build a new life if you have to." Using a walking stick, Drake picked his way along the trail, choosing the smoothest path as possible. "I've gotten a good look at the terrain from the top. Let's go to the end, then if we have time, we can search the offshoots from this canyon. We have five hours of daylight left. We need to be back at the car before sunset."

"You won't get an argument from me. I wouldn't want to be out here in the dark wandering..." She stopped.

Drake slanted a look at Kay. "Did you remember something?"

"I've been here wandering around in the dark, lost but scared to follow the highway. I was purposefully staying away from there."

"Was someone after you?"

"I don't know." Her mouth twisted in frustration. "When am I going to stop saying that?"

"When *we* get to the bottom of this." Drake continued the trek deeper into the canyon.

As he examined the area on the right, she surveyed the left, more questions concerning Kay swirled around in his mind. *What if she isn't Kaleb's mother? What if she stole the baby? What if she's a criminal...*

He shook the thought away. Over the years, he'd learned to read people, usually successfully. He couldn't reconcile the image of Kay being on the run from the law with what he knew. But she could be on the run from someone. What if she got caught up in human trafficking? But if so, where did the baby come from, the locket with her photo and the three hundred dollars she carried?

Kay stared at the tall, rocky facade at the end of the canyon. Fine beads of perspiration coated her face from the exertion of the hike. But suddenly the three-sided limestone walls blocked her view of the wide expanse of sky except for a narrow gap above her. The feel of the chasm closing in on her deluged her senses. Her breathing became rapid. Sweat swathed her and rolled down her face in rivulets.

She'd been here—scared and frantic with night approaching swiftly. And yet there was no sign of a campsite. No shelter at all but a sheer, tall, stony barrier on both sides. She whirled around 180 degrees. Her gaze latched onto the six-foot opening into this part of the canyon, and she started back to the slit.

Drake hurried after her. "Were you here?"

"Yes, but not for long. I would never put myself into such a small space with only one way out."

"How do you know that?"

"Because I'm used to assessing all the ways out of a dangerous situation," she said without any idea where that explanation came from.

"Why?"

She thought about it. Heat and smoke pressing in on her. Flames surrounded her. The sounds of falling beams—the crackling of a fire inundated her. "I've been in a fire and managed to get out."

"That's something I can use to find out who you are. Do you know where?"

She shook her head.

Drake looked at the sky. "Okay. We have time to check out some of those side canyons before we head back to the car."

About two hundred yards into a crevice that started out fifteen feet wide, it narrowed to five feet. "This isn't the one I took, for the same reason as before."

When they started into the second offshoot, the side walls were only about three yards apart. But as Kay continued next to Drake, no alarms went off. When she rounded a bend in the canyon, the area opened up with several large fissures, like spokes in a wheel leading to other possible places.

Kay sighed. "I feel like we are in a maze with so many ways to go we could endlessly wander around."

"Does anything look familiar?"

She rotated slowly, taking in the rocky floor between her and the side of the canyon, hoping to find a clue to her identity. How was she going to protect herself when she didn't know why she was in danger?

Drake clasped her hand and mimicked what she did. His touch shored up her fading optimism that this trip would give her answers.

Halfway around, Kay's gaze fell on a hole in the cliff only a couple of feet off the ground. The gap in the rocks, about four by five feet, drew her forward.

Drake followed, their hands still connected. "The cave? You think you used that?"

"If it had been raining, I would have said yes, but there's something about it that seems familiar." When she stopped at the base of the cave, she swung around, searching the hard-packed earth for a sign she'd been there. Two sets of shoeprints, other than theirs, covered the ground. One boot heel had a distinctive shape.

Drake took photos. "I'll check the cave out, then we need to head back to the car."

As he hoisted himself into the hole, Kay glanced at the sky, still cloud covered, then swept her gaze over the area. She halted, staring at a place directly across the canyon floor with large rocks littering the sandy surface, not far from where she'd entered ten minutes ago. A sense of having done that very same thing nudged her forward. She crossed to the small boulders, most likely from a rock slide, and surveyed the ground. More footprints—some probably hers—trampled the alcove in the cliff.

She approached the pile of small limbs and squatted. Had she gathered them to build a fire at night? In the desert, the temperature would drop quickly and—

She glimpsed a piece of tan canvas wedged between the wall and a large stone. Reaching for what looked like part of a backpack, she chilled as if the temperature had plunged forty degrees in seconds. After clasping the material, she tugged on it, the bag popping out of the hole created by the rock slide.

The feel of it in her hands swamped her with a tidal wave of images. Her watching Kaleb sleeping. The sound of voices coming closer followed by the appearance of two men entering the end of the box canyon. Guns strapped to them. Fierce expressions. Was one of them her assailant in the Cactus Grove jail?

As one of the men climbed into the cave at the end and the other waited, she'd scooped up Kaleb, glanced back to make sure they weren't looking, then, cradling the baby against her, she'd scrambled to get to the crack of the nearby boulder. She'd never make the entrance where she'd come into this section of the canyon. She crammed herself into the slit, sucking in a deep breath while she held Kaleb above her head. He giggled.

She tilted her head back as far as she could, smiled and whispered, "Shh."

She hadn't known how long she'd be able to keep him quiet, so she kept going farther into the rocky fissure. The two men would have a hard time fitting through the slash in the cliff. She paused to listen to where they might be. Voices, speaking Spanish, filled the quiet, growing louder as the two thugs came closer to her hiding place. She pushed deeper into the gap. She tried to follow their heated conversation, but Kaleb began wiggling.

Then the largest guy came into view through the slit. She frantically looked the other way and noted a bend a few feet away. If she could position herself where they couldn't see her and keep Kaleb content, then...

"Kay, where are you?"

She popped up from behind the stones, gripping the backpack in her hand. "I think this is mine." She sidestepped to skirt the large rock.

A rattling sound alerted her to danger. She froze and stared down at the rattlesnake coiled and blocking her way.

SEVEN

"Don't move," Drake said as he brought his rifle up to his shoulder and sighted the reptile down its barrel. "He sees you as a threat. He's just defending himself. If you can, move away slowly. I don't want to shoot him unless he attacks."

Kay took a step away and then several more until she plastered her back against a massive boulder. "That's as far as I can go."

Drake respected the animals he encountered in the wild. "Stay still. I'm coming."

He slid his rifle into its carrying case, then shrugged out of his backpack and retrieved his rope. He slipped his handgun out of its holster. While he kept an eye on the rattlesnake, he scaled the rock next to the bigger boulder, then pulled himself up onto it.

"I'm going to drop down a looped rope. Grab it and hold on."

"Okay," she said in a shaky voice.

When Kay had a secure grip on the twine, Drake laid his gun within reach, then, using his body weight, hoisted Kay up and over the boulder.

When she reached the top, she threw her arms around him. "Thank you. The rattler was guarding the way out." She glanced back. "Now he's decided to leave. He could have ten minutes ago."

"They can be contrary." Chuckling, Drake held her until she stopped trembling, the feel of her in his embrace calming his own fears concerning the snake. He never killed unless he had to. He'd seen enough death and murder in his job. Each time he had walked away from using his gun, he'd felt he'd won a victory against violence.

"Did you see which way he went?"

"Yes. If we keep a wide berth, he'll leave us alone." He glanced at the backpack she held with two water bottles in two side mesh pockets. "Is it yours? Did you look inside?"

"Not yet. I think it's mine. When I touched it, some memories came back."

"Good ones?"

"I was here in this canyon when two men came in. I have the feeling I was running from them, but I don't know for sure. When I saw them, I was trapped until they checked the cave out. I made it to that fissure in the rock and squeezed inside so the men wouldn't see me. It became wider as I moved back."

"How did you get away?"

"I don't know for sure. You called my name, and the images in my mind vanished. The last thing I remember is that I kept creeping through the fissure until it came out into the main canyon. I ran until I couldn't anymore."

"That could have been when you had to take a break and hid where I found you."

"Some of it is sketchy, but the fear I felt wasn't." She folded her arms and rubbed her hands up and down.

Drake unzipped the backpack and set it between them. Inside were baby items, from diapers to wipes, clothes and a handmade blanket.

Kay picked up a stuffed bear and a teething ring. She grazed the soft animal against her cheek, taking a deep sniff of it. A picture of her holding Kaleb teased her thoughts. "This is his favorite toy." She wasn't sure how she knew, but she was sure it was.

Drake took everything out. "There's some more money but no ID. Nothing of yours."

"Maybe I didn't have time to get anything else. I wish I could remember."

He took hold of her hand. "You will. You already are. But you may not ever recall everything. We can bury some memories because they are too hard to deal with."

"That's what I'm afraid of. Something horrific happened and I refuse to remember it."

"Self-preservation can be a strong instinct, but so can a mother protecting her child." What if she'd done something wrong—illegal? He stared at Kay, who was obviously waging a battle with the doubts inside her—evidence of her uncertainties dimmed the light in her eyes; tiny lines of worry around her mouth and on her forehead appeared and clung to her like her tight grip on his hand. A lot of scenarios raced through his mind—none good—but there was a reason he'd stumbled upon her.

God's in control.

"Anna would tell you not to worry. It doesn't do anything but drain your energy and send you in a direction you don't need to go. When my wife was murdered, all I wanted was justice for her. But when her killer was tried and sent to prison for life without parole, it didn't take away the pain I felt without her. I thought once justice had been served, my pain would go away. It didn't, but time has helped me to deal with it."

"But you still feel anger and rage toward her killer."

It was as if she'd delved into the deep recess of his mind and read his innermost thoughts. Was this pain he couldn't let go of holding him in the past? "How can I forgive him? I've managed on most days to forget him but not forgive him."

"I don't know if I could if I was in your shoes." Kay glanced at the sky. "We better leave. I don't want to be here when it's dark."

"Good idea. Follow me down the side of the boulder. There are footholds you can use."

As he made his way to the ground, Drake couldn't shake the feeling he'd let the Lord down. To forgive Shanna's murderer was too high a price to pay. How could he and have peace of mind?

Kay jerked straight up in the front passenger seat of Drake's SUV. For a second confused about where she was, she glanced out the windshield at the dark stretch of road before them. "How long have I been asleep?"

"An hour and a half. You fell asleep not long after we grabbed dinner."

As a car passed them going the opposite way, Kay glimpsed Drake's strong profile in the illumination from the headlights. Even when confronted with a rattlesnake, he'd made her feel safe. "I'm surprised I didn't have a nightmare."

"Your exhaustion finally caught up with you."

"That and I remembered a few things about how I ended up hurt. Did you call the ranch?"

"Yes, earlier, and everything's fine. Anna was thinking about taking Kaleb to see the animals in the barn."

A picture of Kaleb hugging his teddy bear made her smile. "Good. He'll enjoy that. Can I call and see if they are back at the house?"

"Sure. But I wouldn't be surprised if Anna and Kaleb are still at the barn. She likes to take care of my mom's mare. She won't ride, but she loves to pamper Blue Bonnet and groom her."

Kay tried calling, but the line was busy. "Someone must be on the phone. You've piqued my interest in Blue Bonnet. I hope you'll show her to me. I don't know if I've ridden a horse, but they're beautiful animals." She returned his sat phone. "Did you talk with the police or Dallas?"

"I spoke with Dallas and told him what you remembered. He hadn't heard anything from the police yet, but then I didn't think your assailant would suddenly start talking, especially when he asked for a lawyer."

"I guess that would be too easy."

"He isn't going anywhere. Maybe he'll decide to talk soon."

"I'm just glad he was found."

"Do you think he was one of the two men in the canyon?"

"Maybe. I didn't get a great look at their faces close-up. But one had a similar build and coloring as the man in jail. The other was shorter, stockier. And to tell you the truth, my memory of that day is sketchy at best. And there's always the chance it isn't right. I get flashes I can't make sense of." She massaged her temples as though that would make everything clear again. She was missing a large chunk of memory. How did she get to the park? Where did she come from? Why was she out there alone with Kaleb? Even after finding the backpack, she realized she hadn't had the supplies needed to hike and especially to camp out in Big Bend.

"A lot of your flashes are coming when something triggers them. Don't force it."

"Like when you try to remember a person's name you used to know and can't? Then later it just pops into your head?"

"Exactly."

She glanced at the heavier traffic and lights in the distance. "Are we almost to your ranch?"

"Yeah, another ten minutes."

She relaxed and let out a long sigh. "I miss holding Kaleb. This has got to be hard on him. He'll be glad to see Mr. Teddy."

"Mr. Teddy?"

"I figure I'd give the bear a name. Kaleb can't yet."

Drake chuckled. "I like it."

When he turned into the drive that led to his

family home, he scanned the terrain before him and slowed his SUV to a crawl. "Call again."

The stiff tone to his words caused Kay to perk up and sit forward. "What's wrong?" She glanced at the house, where a few lights glowed in the dark.

"Probably nothing, but the Christmas tree is always lit up every night around five o'clock and left on all night. It's a tradition. My father calls it a beacon of light for people who go by on the road."

"They're probably all at the barn and forgot." But when she looked that way, all she saw was one light shining near the main double doors, which was on every night.

"I hope that's it, but something doesn't feel right. My dad and Anna are creatures of habit. If one doesn't turn on the Christmas tree lights, the other does before it grows dark. My mom started it years ago, and they have carried out the tradition since she died." He pulled over to the side of the gravel road. "Call the house again while I get a few things from the back. Stay put. I'll be right back."

She grabbed the sat phone and hit the recent-call button while Drake switched off the head-lights and climbed from the vehicle. Seconds later, he opened the hatch, retrieved something and headed back to the driver's seat with night-vision goggles and his rifle slung over his shoulder.

Again, all she heard was a busy signal. The sight of a second weapon sent her heart racing. Feeling the tension emanating from Drake, she asked, "What's going on? Do you think it's the other guy I remember from the canyon?"

"I don't know, but considering what's been happening lately, I'm not taking any chances. We're going to walk the rest of the way to the house. I'm probably overreacting, but I'd rather be doing that than something unexpected occurring."

"They all could have gone somewhere else." *To hide or flee because of me.* She didn't want to voice that thought out loud, though.

"I told Dallas about the second guy. He's good at his job. If they went somewhere else, it was for a good reason."

"Then why is the phone giving us a busy signal? Why didn't Dallas or your dad call and let you know? We shouldn't have gone. I'm sorry I brought it up."

"You learned a lot more today. All of that may help us piece together what happened. We got back as fast as we could." He twisted toward her.

Although she couldn't see him, she felt the sweep of his gaze, taking her in as though the overhead light shined. She balled her hands, her fingernails stabbing her palms. "I'm coming with you."

"I wasn't going to leave you here, but I want you to stay close. If I tell you to do something, do it without question."

"I will." As though his wary feelings were contagious, a heavy foreboding pressed down on her. "Should we call the police?"

"No, not yet," Drake answered, not wanting to voice his suspicion. What if someone at the police department had leaked Kay's whereabouts? He couldn't take a chance until he figured out what was going on. "C'mon."

He grabbed the sat phone, then put on his night-vision goggles to scan the terrain for anyone before going inside. As he sneaked toward his family home with Kay following, he kept to the dark shadows. He didn't want to enter until he'd circled the house. There were times he hated to think the worst of a situation, but he had to be prepared in case he was right. Being wrong wasn't an option when he was responsible for others' safety.

At the window where the Christmas tree sat, drapes pulled open, he crept up to the sill to peek into the den. One light on the end table dimly illuminated the room. No one was there, which was unusual, because his dad loved to watch television and enjoy the holiday decorations.

"Do you see anything?" Kay whispered close to his ear.

"No. Let's go to the rear deck and enter the house that way." Drake continued his trek toward the kitchen.

As he neared the back door, the silence bothered him more than anything. The only window he'd been able to look inside was the one with the Christmas tree. He paused and swung around, grasping Kay's upper arms. He wanted to leave her outside in case something was wrong, but he couldn't take that risk.

The quiet sharpened his senses as he eased the door open. He entered as though clearing the house of a possible suspect. With gun drawn, he kept it lowered but ready to lift and shoot at a second's notice. After sweeping the kitchen, he crept into the hallway and made his way to the living and dining rooms then the den. Everything was as it should be, except that the Christmas tree lights weren't on. Out of habit, he crossed to the pine in front of the window and plugged the lights in, as if that would make the tightening in his gut go away.

"We'll check your bedroom first, then the rest." Drake moved past Kay.

She clasped his arm and whispered, "Where are they?"

He shrugged his shoulders, not wanting to think of the possibilities. His family knew they were on the way home. Why didn't they call or leave a note? Unless Anna, Kaleb, Dallas, his dad and Frank turned up before they finished going through the house, he would have to call the captain at the police station. Captain Brad Vincent had been a good childhood friend while growing up. Drake would have to trust him.

As he slunk down the hallway, each muscle tightened even more as though he expected an attacker to jump out at any moment. The hairs on his nape stood up, and he forced deep breaths into his lungs.

When he stepped into Kay's bedroom doorway, he stiffened.

Behind him, Kay said, "No!"

He glanced back at her. She cupped her hand over her mouth, her eyes huge. "Let's finish checking the house." He pivoted away from the trashed room with sheets yanked from the bed, drawers emptied and the playpen gone.

"Give me your rifle. I'll stand guard here while you do."

"You know how to shoot?"

"I can pull the trigger if a bad guy comes down this hall." Kay drew up tall, her face set in a look of determination. "I'll do whatever I have to to protect Kaleb."

"I'll be back. Don't take your eyes off the hallway." A steely coldness embedded itself deep in Drake as he continued his search. Someone other than his family and Dallas had been here. Whoever it was would regret ever stepping onto his property.

In his dad's room, he headed straight for the phone on the bedside table. When he picked it up, the line was dead. He retrieved the satellite phone from his pocket and punched in Captain Vincent's number.

"I'm at the ranch. My family, the baby and Texas Ranger Sanders are gone. The house phone is dead, probably the line cut, and one of the rooms is ransacked. I have Kay with me."

"I'll let the sheriff know. I'll be there as soon as I can with a couple of my men, too."

When Drake disconnected the call, he swung around to examine the cold room. His gaze caught a message scrambled on the dresser mirror. "Gone to Mom's peace."

Mom's peace? He continued his survey, discovering the source of the chill. The door to the deck was ajar. Had someone gotten in this way, or had his dad left through this exit? He carefully swung the opening wider without touching the knob and peered outside into the darkness.

As he stepped back into the house, his attention fixed on several drops of what looked like blood on the tiles by the entry.

EIGHT

Kay kept her focus on the corridor. She'd told Drake she could use the rifle. She'd said it before she even thought about what that meant. Maybe she did know how to shoot. Either way, she wouldn't let whoever was after her win. If Kaleb had been kidnapped, she wouldn't rest until she found him. She hadn't hiked for miles carrying him to let him be taken from her.

Another memory teased the edges of her mind. The mist cleared, giving her a picture of herself standing at a shooting range holding a handgun and firing.

For a second, she sliced her gaze toward the upheaval in the guest bedroom. Were they looking for something besides Kaleb? As she started to return her attention to the hallway, she glimpsed a small hole in the wall near the dresser.

A bullet hole!

She gasped and faced forward. She wished

Drake was back. What if someone was still in the house? Throwing a quick peek at the corner he'd disappeared around, she fortified herself with a newly discovered resolve. She didn't give up easily.

"I'm coming back, Kay."

As the sound of his footsteps grew closer, she relaxed the tight muscles in her arms and brought the rifle down. "I have something to show you."

"Me, too."

"What?"

"You first, then we need to check out the garage. Dallas's truck is still here and Frank's is by the barn, but what about Anna's or my father's vehicles?" He stopped only a foot from her.

Every time she saw him, her heart kicked up a notch. The strong planes of his face and his muscular build reassured her he could protect her. That eased the panic surging at the sight of the bullet hole.

She turned and pointed at it. "Something more than trashing the place went on here."

"In my dad's room, I found the deck door open and blood on the floor, leading outside. I followed a trail, and it went across the deck and down the steps."

"You think your dad was shot?"

"Could be. His pistol is gone. He could have been defending himself."

Drake entered the room and examined the hole in the wall by the dresser on the far side. "There's blood here, too." He faced her. "I called the police. Help is on the way. Let's see if any vehicles are gone from the garage."

When they reached the door to the garage, Kay recalled the first time she'd been in it, when Drake had brought her home after the assailant tried to kidnap Kaleb in the field. "Drake, I think Kaleb is at the center of this."

"Why?"

"Because behind the café, my attacker tried to take Kaleb from me. Maybe someone is trying to kidnap him, and I've been on the run, trying to prevent that."

"That could be what happened. Usually in a baby snatching, there's a reason, like ransom or baby trafficking. If it was for a reason like ransom, I could see them pursuing you, especially if someone paid them, but in baby trafficking, I doubt they would have gone to all that trouble. They would find an easier target."

For ransom? That usually meant a person had money to pay it. If she came from a wealthy family, why wasn't it broadcast that she and Kaleb were missing? Not much made sense to Kay, and when she thought about it, her head usually began to throb with all the questions. There was no time to deal with them right now. They had to find Kaleb and Drake's family.

He reached for the rifle in her hands.

"No, you can't shoot both weapons at the same time. While standing guard, I had a memory of being at a shooting range. I know my way around a gun."

"Until I see your ability with a gun, I'm taking both. Stay behind me." He moved toward the kitchen.

She couldn't blame Drake for insisting he keep the weapons, but Kaleb was hers, and she needed to be involved in protecting him. She held her breath as he flipped the switch and opened the door to the garage. When he stepped down onto the concrete floor, Kay glimpsed both Anna's and Tom's vehicles.

"Stay here. I'm going to check around."

When Drake returned from his search of the garage, grim lines cut deep into his expression. "Either they were taken or—" he passed her in the entrance and walked across the kitchen "—they're hiding somewhere on the ranch."

She hurried after him as he left by the back door and strode toward the barn, his gaze sweeping the terrain around them the whole time.

Halfway to the barn, Drake stopped. "'Mom's

peace' was written across my dad's dresser mirror."

"What's that mean?"

"Mom loved riding Blue Bonnet when she had a problem to work out, but I don't think that's it. That's too obvious." He pivoted and headed in the direction they'd come from. When he reached the yard, he made his way toward a garden in the back with lush bushes in the center. "If they're anywhere, it's the bomb shelter."

"A bomb shelter like from the Cold War?"

"Yep. My granddaddy had it installed in the early 1950s. Since then, it's come in handy a few times for a tornado warning. It's not common knowledge."

A shot rang out in the still of night. Kay reacted as though she'd been fired upon before. She dived behind a large brick barbecue grill while Drake ducked around a matching three-foot brick wall.

"Are you all right?" Drake rose partway and returned fire.

"Yes. How about you?"

"Stay down. The shot came from the barn. The police will arrive any minute."

He didn't answer her question. Had he been hurt? He'd jerked to the left when she heard the shot. Keeping the brick structure between herself and the barn, she sidled along it until she could see Drake in the dim light from the house.

"Where were you hit?"

"It's nothing," he said as a bullet struck the top of the wall near him, chunks of brick flying in the air. He crawled toward Kay until he could stand up, using the outdoor grill as his shield.

Sirens in the distance reverberated in the quiet.

Immediately Kay saw the blood seeping through Drake's jacket from a wound on his upper left arm. She reached for the rifle. "At least let me have a weapon."

"I don't think—"

Another shot sounded, hitting where Drake had been a moment before. As a man flung open the rear barn door and ran, Kay took the rifle, aimed and fired.

Kay struck a leg, and the man went down while a second intruder left his shelter, firing two handguns toward them. She flattened herself behind the barbecue grill. From the other side, Drake discharged his weapon twice.

The man on the ground started crawling away. His comrade disappeared around the side of the barn, shielded from them, and fired his weapon again.

The police couldn't be more than half a mile away.

"I'm not letting the hurt man get away. Keep a lookout while I catch him." Drake charged forward across the ground between the yard and where one of the shooters grasped the wooden slat of a fence.

As Drake raced toward the hurt man, Kay kept vigilant for the other intruder. The sirens grew even louder. Then she caught sight of multiple headlights coming down the gravel road. When several stopped not far from her, she hurried toward the first officer, who exited his car.

"Drop the gun, ma'am," he said, raising his.

She hadn't even realized she still held the rifle. She immediately followed his directions. "I'm Kay. Texas Ranger Jackson is securing one of the gunmen behind the barn." She pointed in the direction. "Another man fled around the far side of the barn. Probably halfway across the field by now."

Captain Brad Vincent approached them. "Officer Thomas, go help him."

"Yes, sir."

"Dispatch the other officers to search the field

on the east side of the barn." After his man left, he faced Kay. "Are you all right?"

"I am, but Drake has been shot. According to him, it's nothing."

A brief smile flashed across the captain's mouth. "Knowing Drake, that doesn't surprise me."

More patrol cars drove toward the house, along with an ambulance, probably because Drake had told them he had found a blood trail. The adrenaline that had pounded through her during the skirmish slowly subsided, and all she wanted to do was sink to the ground. She didn't. She still had to find Kaleb.

Crack!

The captain shoved Kay to the ground while drawing his firearm and turning toward the sound of the gunshot. In the distance, she heard what she thought were the police officers in the field returning fire.

She immediately searched for Drake at the back of the barn with the downed suspect. A surge of adrenaline flooded her body again. Drake knelt next to the wounded attacker on the ground. Earlier he'd been trying to get away, but now he was still, his head rolling to the side. Had the man been shot by his partner?

When it quieted down, she lifted her head to get a better sense of what was going on. The ambulance pulled up near the rear of the barn while sheriff's deputies came to the aid of the police officers hunting the other assailant in the field.

When Captain Vincent received a radio call, he answered, "Let the sheriff's deputies take over. We still need to find the family and secure the area." After disconnecting, the man swiveled around and extended a hand to help her up. "The other suspect was killed in the field."

The viciousness of the past half hour overwhelmed Kay. As she rose, her legs shook, and she wasn't sure she could even walk. She glanced toward the back of the barn and saw the paramedics lift the intruder onto the gurney, then cover his body, including his head, with a sheet. Two men had died tonight. What was going on? So much violence, all because of her, and she couldn't even give a reason why. She hugged her arms to her chest, trying to ward off the chill that encased her. But it drilled deep into her bones.

Lord, I have to remember more than bits and pieces. How can I protect Kaleb when I don't know who's behind this?

Drake stopped long enough to let a paramedic bandage his upper arm where a bullet had grazed him. It hurt, but he didn't have time to go to the hospital, as the EMT suggested. He'd had worse wounds than this one.

He scanned for Kay. When he spotted her twenty yards away near the police captain, the light from the back deck illuminated her face. For a few seconds, he thought she'd gone into shock. Even from a distance, he could see she was trembling, and the normal rosy hue was gone from her cheeks.

He strode toward Kay and Brad, who ended a radio call as he approached. "What happened in the field?"

Brad frowned. "Once the gun went off, my guys knew where the suspect was and cornered him. He wouldn't surrender. He kept firing."

Drake wasn't surprised he was the first to arrive. Growing up, he and Brad had lived on neighboring ranches and had done everything together. His position at the police department had made Drake's transition to his new post in Cactus Grove even easier. "I think Dad and the others are in the bomb shelter." He and Drake used to play in the shelter until one day when the door became stuck and they couldn't get out. Hearing their pounding and screams, his father had found them an hour later.

"I'll be with you in a moment. I want my men to check the house thoroughly and the grounds around it. I don't want any more surprises."

"Neither do I. I thought I was a goner when I heard the shot, but then I saw the assailant hit." When he heard Kay suck in a deep breath, he didn't say he'd thought the guy in the field would fire again and he had been looking for a place to protect himself. As Brad walked away, Drake took her hand. "I'm fine, and I'm sure Dad had everyone hide in the bomb shelter. It fit the message in his handwriting on his mirror. Mom referred to it as her place of peace ever since she and Dad hid in it during a tornado. Lots of damage to the ranch, but they were all right. Let's go tell them it's safe now."

"Is it?" Kay asked, her voice quavering.

He slowed and faced her. "For the moment."

"I can't put your family at risk anymore."

"With all the law enforcement officers crawling around, anyone who stuck around is a fool. We have options. We'll talk later." He wanted to give her hope, but he felt he was navigating a maze blind. "I'm not backing out because of this. We have a few leads to work on, and today you remembered more."

"I'm not sure it's the same person, but the guy behind the barn fit the build of the second hiker in the canyon."

"I wondered if one of the two men had also been in the park. I intend to press the assailant we have in jail. He won't know that man was murdered by his partner." Drake started forward again. "No doubt Dallas heard the gunshots and is wondering what happened."

Kay's gaze connected with his. "I can't wait to hold Kaleb again."

When Drake pulled on the handle a half minute later, he couldn't lift the heavy door of the bomb shelter. It was locked from the inside, which meant his family was down there. He pounded on the metal door. "Dallas, it's Drake. It's all clear."

The sound of a latch sliding back sent relief through Drake, overriding the throbbing in his arm. He'd been ninety percent sure that was where they were, but it was so much better knowing for sure.

Dallas popped up from the hole, took one look at Kay and immediately said, "Kaleb and everyone are fine. Thanks to Tom's quick thinking and actions."

Drake and Kay moved away from the opening to allow everyone to climb out of the shelter. Tears ran down her face. But when Anna appeared holding Kaleb, a huge smile graced Kay's mouth.

She took her baby from Drake's cousin and enveloped the child in her embrace. "Thank you all for protecting Kaleb." More tears flowed from her eyes as she pressed her baby against her chest.

His dad surveyed the ranch, his attention lingering on all the police vehicles still there. "We heard the shooting. What happened here?"

"That's what I want to know from you," Drake said and began walking toward the house. "But I'd feel better going into the house, where we aren't sitting ducks."

"Me, too." Kay accompanied Drake, increasing her stride to keep up.

"You'll get no argument from me." Frank passed Drake and entered the kitchen first.

A few minutes later all of them, except Anna, sat in the den with every drape pulled shut. Brad and the sheriff would join them later. Kay gave Kaleb a bottle and held him while he drank. No one said anything until Anna finally came into the room with a tray of mugs, filled with coffee.

After she handed out the drinks and took a lounge chair, Drake finally asked the question he'd wanted answered a while ago. "What happened here?"

Dallas took a sip of his coffee. "When we returned from the barn, your dad was the first into the house. He shot an intruder in Kay's bedroom. The assailant returned fire and fled down the hall to your dad's room. He escaped out the door onto the back deck."

Drake's father put his mug on a coaster. "And it looked like he was calling or radioing someone as he fled. That's when we put into motion the plan Dallas came up with right after you two left, in case the place was attacked. Taking the car wasn't an option, because most likely whoever came with the intruder had an eye on the way out of the ranch, possibly even set up an ambush. We retreated to the bomb shelter. We took the playpen for Kaleb. We didn't know how long we would be down there."

"I tried to call the police while the men snatched what we would need with Kaleb." Anna shook her head. "The line was dead. How did you get the police here?"

"The sat phone I took with me. Thankfully, it worked. There were areas in the canyon where it didn't." Drake looked at Kay, who cradled Kaleb against her and held the bottle for him as he nodded off. The sight stirred his heart, and he realized in a short time she had become important to him, as had the baby. "I'm glad someone can go to sleep. How did the assailants know Kay and Kaleb were here? It's not like we've ever used our home as a safe house before."

Frank and his dad shook their heads while Dallas said, "Don't know for sure, but if someone was desperate enough, he would check all possibilities out, and you were working the case."

"Who trashed the bedroom Kay and Kaleb are staying in?" Drake asked the group while his gaze strayed again to Kay. She set the empty bottle on the end table, then finally relaxed back against the couch cushion, but tension still held her expression, her lips pinched together, her jaw set in a firm line.

"It wasn't us, but the guy I shot." Frank rubbed his nape. "He must have been looking for something."

"What? I only had the clothes I had on when I was in the canyon." She straightened forward, jostling Kaleb enough that he fussed for a few seconds before settling back into sleep.

"What about the backpack we found today?" Drake hated the fact he couldn't end this nightmare for Kay and Kaleb.

"Y'all found some of Kay's belongings?" Dallas stood. "Where are they? Maybe something is in there that they wanted."

"It's in the back of my SUV halfway down the gravel road."

"I'll get it. I need to talk with the sheriff." Dallas left the den.

"The only things in the backpack are for Kaleb—clothes to a few toys. In fact, Mr. Teddy is one of the toys. I think it's one of Kaleb's favorites." Kay sipped her coffee. "Maybe the intruder was angry because no one was in the house and trashed the bedroom."

Drake locked gazes with her. "We'll figure it out."

"I hope so. I'm remembering bits and pieces, but I still don't know who I am or why this is happening to me."

Brad poked his head through the doorway. "Can I have a word with you, Drake?"

"Sure." He rose. His gut roiled with an uneasy feeling. Brad wore his neutral expression, the one he used when he had grave information.

Out in the hallway, Drake moved Brad away from the entrance into the den. Whatever he had to tell him, he didn't want the others to overhear it. Kay was putting up a brave front, but Drake was worried about her. Just inside the kitchen, he pivoted. "Spill it."

"The suspect who hasn't been talking to us was found dead in his cell tonight."

NINE

Sitting in the den with Drake's family, Kay tried to push away the feelings that had bombarded her during the past hour. She couldn't. They had a stranglehold on her, intent on choking off her resolution to discover how and why she and Kaleb had ended up in Big Bend National Park. They threatened to cripple her ability to fight for her real life back. For a few moments while bullets had struck the brick nearby, she'd wanted to surrender. Maybe then she would find answers to the blank slate of memories in her mind.

What if every image or memory she'd thought was real wasn't? Kaleb's name? Childhood remembrances? But when she said she could shoot a gun, she'd been right. She'd wounded an intruder. The numbness she'd encased the incident in suddenly fell away, and whatever led her to this point vanished.

Chilled, with tremors rippling down her body, she clasped her hands together to keep the others from seeing her fall apart. Kay glanced at Kaleb, now in Anna's arms, and shot to her feet. "Excuse me."

Before they could ask what was wrong, she fled the room, seeking the bathroom. But instead, she came to halt as the captain left the kitchen and passed her in the hallway. She nodded at him, then glanced toward Drake in the doorway. He was assessing her.

He knew what she was feeling. She saw it in his eyes. She couldn't move, as though a blizzard had flash frozen her.

He covered the space between them and took one of her trembling hands, then drew her toward the kitchen. The compassion in his expression urged her forward, as if he'd offer her a haven from all that had happened in less than a week.

Exhaustion prodded her toward the table. She sat. Drake pulled out the chair next to her and eased down onto it.

"It must be bad if you're talking to me alone in here. What did the captain want?" Kay leaned back, trying to relax her tensed muscles. She couldn't.

Drake covered her hand near him. "The man in jail was found dead tonight in his cell."

"Someone killed him? How?"

"There are no visible signs, but Brad thinks he

might have been poisoned. He'll know for sure after the autopsy."

"So he doesn't think it's from natural causes?"

Drake shook his head. "As to the how he got hold of a poison in jail, not sure. What the poison is might help us answer that question. Some cause death quickly while others don't."

"Do you think he was poisoned to keep him quiet?"

"That's the most likely answer to why."

"Just like the assailant in the field earlier killed his partner. We don't have any leads to follow." Kay dropped her head and closed her eyes, trying to digest the latest news and its implication. What in the world was she in the middle of? She willed herself to remember—anything that would help them—but nothing came to her.

"You and Kaleb can't stay here."

She lifted her head, disappointment warring with anger. "I certainly understand. You can't put your family in danger. I appreciate what you've done for us. Will one of the deputy sheriffs drive Kaleb and me into Cactus Grove?"

Drake's eyebrows slashed downward. "Why do you want to do that?"

"You said we shouldn't stay here."

"You aren't going anywhere without me. I made a promise to you—and Kaleb. You are *not* alone in this. What kind of person would I be if I kicked you out of my house at a time like this? I could never live with myself if something happened to you. I thought you knew me well enough to know that."

Tears filled her eyes. "But this isn't your problem. Tonight your family was put in danger because of me. I don't have a right to ask that of you." A tear track ran down her face.

Drake scooted his chair over until his left side pressed against her, then he encircled her in his embrace and drew her toward him. "We're in this together. And I'm not going to tell you that again. Just believe it. I'm not walking away from you or Kaleb."

"But your dad, Anna—"

He laid his fingers over her mouth. "Two deputy sheriffs are staying outside on guard tonight, then tomorrow we're leaving. Dallas has a place we can go where we should be safe. He'll be staying, too, until we get to the bottom of this."

"I… I…can't let—"

Drake cupped her face and covered her mouth with his. His gentle kiss drove all thoughts from her mind. All her focus narrowed to the feel of his lips on hers. Coaxing. Persuading her to give in to the feelings she'd held in check ever since she opened her eyes and looked up into his in the park.

When he leaned back, breaking their connection, bereavement swept through her. For one brief moment, she'd forgotten all her worries. Now they returned in full force.

He brushed his fingers along her cheek, hooking stray strands of hair behind her ear. "My family will be all right. They've decided to visit my grandparents in the Florida Panhandle, and if they have to, they'll stay for Christmas. They're leaving tomorrow at the same time we do."

"But what are you going to do about the holidays with your family?"

"If this hasn't been solved by then, we'll celebrate some other time. It won't be the first Christmas I missed with my family. Besides, the twenty-fifth is a couple of weeks away." He cocked a grin. "But I don't plan for this to go on that long."

Dallas and Frank came into the kitchen and headed for the rear door.

"Where are y'all going?" Drake asked, reclining in his chair.

Dallas paused at the exit. "Kaleb will need his playpen. We left some other items in the bomb shelter, too. We decided we'll all camp out in the den for the night."

"You know, safety in numbers." A smile flittered across Frank's face, but it waned quickly.

When the door closed behind the two men, Kay drew in a composing breath and centered her thoughts on the positive. Negative thinking would only drag her down. God was in control. He wouldn't give her more than she could handle. She did have help. She wasn't alone in dealing with the assailants. *Thank You, Lord, for sending Drake.*

As the sun kissed the western horizon the next afternoon, Drake held up his binoculars and scanned the flat desert terrain surrounding the cabin where he, Kay, Kaleb and Dallas would stay. One of Dallas's distant cousins owned the cabin and wasn't using it right now. To be on the safe side, Dallas had taken the long way to their new refuge. The immediate land around it was flat, with few places someone could hide. To the west about four hundred yards away were low, gently rolling hills. The only other building on the property was a detached shed where they had stashed his SUV.

The sat phone worked here, so they had a way to call for help if they needed it. No one knew where they were, not even the police in Cactus Grove. He'd arranged for Texas Ranger Ian Pierce in the El Paso office to gather information about the progress of the case; when Drake called in, Ian would update him so they could continue trying to figure out what was going on.

The sound of the door opening behind him

caused him to turn in that direction. Dallas exited the cabin to begin his four-hour shift standing guard.

Drake swept the landscape one last time before going inside, passing the high-powered binoculars to Dallas. "Boy, time flies when you're having such a good time."

Dallas chuckled. "Essentially this is a stakeout, and that's always been my least favorite part of our job."

"Me, too. I did a walk around about fifteen minutes ago," he said, then went into the cabin through the only door.

Drake hadn't realized how cold it was outside because of the wind that blew in from the northwest until he shut the door and the toasty warmth of the interior enticed him toward the blaze going in a large fireplace. A mouthwatering scent hung in the air. Dinner? On the way to the cabin, Dallas had gone inside a convenience store and bought supplies from a list they had all contributed to.

Slowly Drake turned in a circle. Where were Kay and Kaleb? He hadn't realized how much he'd been looking forward to seeing her until he found the main area empty. He'd made it a point never to become emotionally involved with a case, but somehow in the past several days, he had. Last night during the shootout, he'd realized he couldn't dismiss his feelings any longer, which was a big problem for him.

The only thing he should be concerned about was protecting her and Kaleb. Nothing should be allowed to divert his attention. But all she had to do was smile at him and something shifted deep inside him, making a mockery of his decision only to concentrate on his job. A noise to his right drew him around to face Kay emerging from the only bedroom in the small cabin.

She quietly shut the door and grinned at him. "Kaleb is finally taking a nap. He fought it for hours. Too much going on, but exhaustion won out in the end. Would you like me to fix more coffee? Dallas finished the last bit left in the pot."

"Yes, that would be perfect. Something smells great. Dinner?"

"Chili seems to be a dish I know how to make, but I have no idea where my recipe came from." Frustration laced her voice as she fixed more coffee.

"I've never lost my memory, but I can imagine how hard that is on you."

She stirred the large pot on the stove. "What if I'm having false memories?"

"What you remembered in the park helped us find your backpack."

"But it didn't help us."

"How about Mr. Teddy? Kaleb has been clutching it since you gave it to him."

"True." She came into the main room, carrying two mugs. "But I wanted to find my driver's license or some other form of ID. Why didn't I have my license with me, and yet I have items that were obviously for Kaleb? Nothing for myself."

If she'd run away on the spur of the moment, he could see her grabbing what she could for the baby first. But then where had the money come from? Most people didn't carry that kind of money around unless they were planning a trip. Drake grabbed his coffee from her outstretched hand and then sat at one end of the worn brown leather couch, hoping she took the seat next to him.

Stop thinking about what can't be! He was on duty and had never had any intention of getting seriously involved with another woman besides Shanna.

He drank a gulp of the hot liquid and almost spewed it out. Instead he swallowed it and put the mug on the end table. Kay eased down at the other end of the sofa, thankfully oblivious to his scalding mouth. What was it about Kay that drew him? Made him do things he didn't normally do?

"What if Kaleb isn't my son? What if—"

"Then why hasn't there been an Amber Alert put out on him?" Drake asked before she let her doubt interfere with whatever she would remember in the future. "I've checked across the country and beyond our borders. There's nothing about a baby that fits his description. When you put pressure on yourself, it can stifle you."

"And you need me to remember."

"Yes. I've seen you and Kaleb together. He isn't afraid of you. In fact, when he's upset, you're the only one who can calm him down. I've never had children, but that tells me there's a connection between you—like a mother and son." For a few seconds, all the regret and sorrow he'd experienced when the medical examiner had told him Shanna had been pregnant when she was murdered inundated him. They had wanted a family.

"I feel that way, too. I'm just getting desperate, especially after what happened last night at your ranch."

"Trust yourself." Drake cradled his mug, and this time he slowly sipped his cooler coffee. His gaze fell on an unopened carton Anna and his dad had given them before leaving. "I thought you and Dallas would have looked at what was inside the box."

"I was going to, but Kaleb took up all my time. He's been fussier than usual. Not much pleases him. Even Mr. Teddy and holding him weren't enough until he exhausted himself."

"He could be teething."

"I checked his mouth. I couldn't see or feel anything to indicate that."

"He's probably sensing all our tension."

"Maybe. I thought of that, too, so I'm trying to be as calm as possible when holding him. Hopefully he'll be better after he gets some sleep." Kay waved her hand toward the carton. "In the meantime, we should see what's inside." For a moment, excitement lit her eyes.

"Go for it." He handed her his pocketknife.

She slit the tape on the top and flipped the lids back. Her gaze widened. "A miniature Christmas tree." She lifted it out of the box and set it on the coffee table, then plunged her hand back inside and brought out another small box. When she opened it, she smiled. "Leave it to Anna to think of everything. These are the decorations for the tree."

"I'd forgotten we hadn't put that one up yet this year. My father bought it for my mother my first Christmas. I was crawling and a little terror. She was afraid I'd pull the big tree down and get hurt."

"At least Kaleb isn't crawling, although his scooching on the floor could cause trouble. I've put some items out of his reach. I hope I thought of everything." Kay scanned the room, rose and took a small trash can and set it up higher.

"Let's have some chili, then put the ornaments on the tree. It'll brighten up the cabin."

"And make this place feel more like a home than a hideaway. Stay right there." She headed for the kitchen. "I'll bring you a bowl, then we'll do what we can to this cabin."

While Kay fixed their dinner, Drake relaxed against the couch cushion and closed his eyes, letting his tension siphon from him—at least for a while, or he would never catch any z's before his next guard duty shift.

A picture of Kay hiding from the assailants the night before appeared in his mind and wouldn't go away. She'd been brave, but in her expression, he'd seen the fear. He remembered that same look on his mother's face when he'd been eight years old and the new bull charged him in the field. His mom had managed to catch the angry animal's attention, which allowed him to flee the paddock and then watch her race for the fence. The bull struck the wooden planks as his mother scrambled over the enclosure, one horn grazing her calf.

He couldn't allow the time he spent with Kay doing normal activities to lure him into a sense of safety. Like that bull, whoever was after her and Kaleb could appear at any time. Drake sat forward, resting his elbows on his thighs and clasping his hands tightly. His actions as a child had nearly caused his mother to be gored badly by a charging sixteen-hundred-pound machine. He needed to distance himself from Kay emotionally, but as she returned to the main room, carrying a tray with two bowls and crackers, her gaze found his, and for that moment there wasn't any fear. Instead, a soft glow radiated from her.

He was in trouble.

While Drake slept in the bedroom with Kaleb, Kay sat on the couch, staring at the three-foot Christmas tree in the center of the table—half in the kitchen and half in the living room. The miniature ornaments sparkled and glittered, a festive touch in a trying time.

Would her life ever return to normal? What was normal for her? She kept pushing herself to remember, and for a few seconds, she would think she was within grasp of a memory. But then she'd hit a dark wall and lean back to find its top. There was no end to the barrier. Ever since she arrived at the cabin eight hours ago, there had been no memories or feelings about her past, whereas before she'd been receiving some. Did she have to be in danger to remember? Was she blocking the truth from herself?

She looked again at the Christmas tree as

though the answers were somewhere on it. The twinkling lights mesmerized her, urging her to go to sleep. She blinked and dragged her attention away. She would sleep when Drake went outside to relieve Dallas. Maybe when she was totally relaxed and sleeping, something would come to her. Remembering her past could be the difference between safety and death for her and Kaleb.

It wasn't even nine o'clock, but she couldn't keep her eyes open. She'd insisted that Drake sleep on the bed because an hour ago she couldn't image herself resting yet. She'd been wound so tightly that she'd used the time Drake had gone into the bedroom to clean and finish putting up the few decorations Anna had given them besides the tree and ornaments.

Now she was surrounded with Christmas, and she couldn't remember anything about the traditions she had at this time of year. Maybe she should grab some shut-eye. She could be interrupted with a...

Something teased her thoughts. A memory. She couldn't quite put it together.

She fixed her attention on the garland hanging from the mantel over the fireplace. Slowly she dropped her gaze to the dying flames in the grate. She rose and snatched a log to add to the fire, then another. Sparks shot upward, and crackles sounded. A blaze flared with the additional fuel. When she put another piece of wood on top, waves of heat enveloped her.

The sensation sent her to her knees. She gripped a fireplace stone as visions paraded across her mind. Red-hot flames surrounded her, dancing closer and closer to her. *Trapped.* Calling for help, she spun around, trying to find a way out. A break in the inferno beckoned her. She hurried toward it, only to have each end race to meet the other.

Kay jumped to her feet, swinging away from the fireplace.

The memory vanished, and all she saw was Drake crossing the room to her, deep lines of concern etched into his face. He clasped her upper arms. "Are you okay?"

She nodded.

"Did you remember something that'll help us?"

"I'm not sure what it was."

He urged her toward the couch and sat as she did—right next to her, his thigh touching hers. "Tell me about it."

His nearness soothed her taut nerves. "I was trapped in the middle of a raging fire. Then I saw a way out, but it was quickly disappearing."

"Did you escape?"

She attempted a smile that quivered. "Apparently, I did, if it was a real memory." She waved her hand down her length. "But I don't know if it really has anything to do with why I was in Big Bend with Kaleb."

"Or something else?"

"Yes, from my past or totally made up. It happened when I was putting more logs on the dying fire."

"So you think it was the power of suggestion that produced the memory?"

"Maybe. It might have nothing to do with my past."

"Or everything. Remember you told me you'd been in a fire before. Maybe the two memories are connected."

"I'll never take for granted remembering my past or the importance of it. I feel like I'm living with a stranger in my head. We're who we are because of all our previous experiences. People draw on their prior knowledge to help them make decisions. It becomes difficult when you don't remember those experiences. What's stopping me from recalling what happened to me? My head doesn't hurt anymore, and even the scrapes and bruises I suffered are starting to disappear."

"Your mind can block memories of a traumatic event to protect you from pain and suffering."

Kay dropped her head and scrubbed her hands

down her face. "All the more reason I shouldn't forget what it was. It's obvious with those men after me it's something dangerous—at least to me and Kaleb."

"Turn around. You'll never get any sleep if you don't relax." He ran his fingers down her neck. "You're coiled tighter than a boa constrictor around its prey."

She did as he asked, a deep throbbing ache along her shoulders, the muscles twisted into a knotted ball. When he began kneading the soreness away, her eyes slid closed. She willed the tension from her body, and slowly, as he worked, she truly relaxed for the first time in days. She hadn't thought that would be possible, especially after last night. Something traumatic had most likely happened to her, causing her to be injured in Big Bend. She'd blocked that from her mind, but she remembered every second of the shootout at the ranch and the assailant coming after her behind the café. What memory was worse than those incidents?

"You're tightening up again. Relax. Think about good things."

"Isn't that kinda hard when you've forgotten your past?"

He chuckled, the soft sound producing a grin from Kay. "There. Keep doing whatever you're doing now."

Thinking about Drake. Dangerous. How could she have feelings for him when she couldn't even remember who she was? She couldn't explain why she knew she wasn't married—that she didn't have anyone in her life except Kaleb.

Before she tensed again, she focused on the sweet baby boy in the other room. He'd been a trouper through the past days, although this afternoon nothing had pleased him. Poor Dallas had gotten little rest before he'd relieved Drake outside. She was glad she'd finally gotten Kaleb to sleep.

Drake stopped massaging her shoulders. "That should help you a little."

"More than a little," Kay said as she twisted toward him.

He was so near, their faces only inches away from each other. His intense expression, focused totally on her, seized her attention and held it captive. Their breaths tangled. He tilted his head closer.

She wanted him to kiss her again. Anticipated it.

TEN

Drake couldn't drag his gaze away from Kay's mouth. He wanted to kiss her again.

No, I shouldn't.

Those words screamed through his mind, taunting him. He shouldn't have before. She was vulnerable. He couldn't lose focus on his main task: protecting her and Kaleb.

For a long moment, he hovered suspended between kissing her and pulling away—doing the right thing. A battle raged inside him, and it took all his willpower to slide his hands away from her and lean back.

Her forehead furrowed as two patches of red colored her cheeks. The urge to cup her face and explain his dilemma was strong. But the closer they became, the harder it would be to deal with her situation objectively. Because in the past few days, he'd realized one thing: whatever Kay was involved in wouldn't go away, and someone out there wanted to kill her and take Kaleb. He hadn't been looking at her circumstances as a police officer but as a man attracted to her. He was missing something vital that might mean the difference between life and death.

He surged to his feet. "I need to relieve Dallas." He started for the door, snatching his overcoat from a peg.

"You still have half an hour. Stay and rest. I'm going to bed."

At the door, he glanced over his shoulder. "That's okay. I need to call the captain and see what's going on in Cactus Grove, especially concerning the death at the jail."

The hurt in her eyes pierced his heart. She covered the distance to the bedroom door, quietly opened it and slipped inside—without a word.

He felt the knife in his heart twist even more.

He stalked outside before he made another mistake and sought to explain how he couldn't care for someone and lose her like he had his wife. He'd barely pulled himself together after her murder and the loss of their unborn child.

He dug deep for his professional mantle—for Kay's sake and his.

Cold air embraced him with icy arms. In a few hours, the temperature had dropped at least thirty degrees.

Drake strode toward Dallas. "Have you heard from the El Paso office?"

"Nope."

"Then I'll give Brad a call and see if he has any news about the suspect's death. He didn't seem like a guy who would kill himself." Drake took the sat phone from his partner. "Kay and Kaleb are in the bedroom."

"Was Kaleb asleep while I was out here?"

"Yes. Why?"

"Because he wasn't a happy camper earlier. I didn't think Kay would be able to get him down. Poor little guy. He must be having a hard time understanding what's going on."

"Or he does and doesn't like it," Drake said with a chuckle. "If I were in his shoes, that would be how I would deal with all the chaos."

Dallas headed for the cabin. "I'll relieve you in four hours."

The nearly full moon brightened the landscape, but not enough. Once Drake had finished talking to Brad, he would use his night-vision binoculars and circle the cabin, panning the terrain from all angles.

Drake made his call to the police captain.

"I assume y'all are settled in," Brad said, a little out of breath.

"Yes. Is everything okay?"

"Yes and no. I got the autopsy on our unknown suspect who died in jail last night, but the results only bring up more questions."

"How did he die?" Drake began a slow sweep of the landscape.

"Cyanide poisoning, although it wasn't from what he ate or drank at dinner. His death was hours after that, and cyanide acts fast."

"He killed himself?" Drake whispered, trying to run through all the scenarios in his mind.

"There were no signs that he was forced to take the cyanide by someone else. In fact, I don't see anyone forcing that big guy to kill himself. He was thoroughly searched when he arrived at the police station before questioning."

"What if he decided to commit suicide because that was expected of him if he was caught? Remember how the other two that came to the ranch ended up dead. One of them killed the other, then went down in a shootout."

"Which means we can't get any information from them."

"Yeah. Who has that kind of sway over a person?" As Drake proposed the question, the ruthless heads of a few criminal organizations immediately came to mind.

"The head of a drug cartel."

"Possibly." How did Kay get mixed up in a drug cartel? "But even more important, how did our suspect get the cyanide, probably a pill, to kill himself if he was thoroughly searched when he was brought in?"

"As you know, that's protocol, and when not being interviewed, he was kept in a cell by himself."

"Start there. Someone breached your security." Drake made his way to the side of the cabin.

"The only people he talked to were his lawyer and my personnel..." Brad sighed. "I'll look into this personally."

"Keep me informed." When Drake disconnected from the police captain, he couldn't shake his earlier question: *How did Kay get mixed up in a drug cartel?*

Kay stumbled through the gap in the fire, the smoke so thick she felt turned around. *Where am I?*

She knelt and scrambled forward. Visibility near the floor was a couple of feet in front of her. A crash behind her prodded her even faster. While glancing back to see what happened, she continued to crawl in what she prayed was the direction out.

As she returned her attention ahead of her, she ran into a still body. She grabbed the little girl and dragged her toward a door.

Into a hallway where flames raced in her direction. She scanned for another way out, but sweat pouring down her face made it difficult to see through the...

Kay's eyes opened, staring at the darkness. Or was she still dreaming? It took a moment to realize she was in a cabin. She turned her head and, through the dimness caused by a slit of light under the door, she spied the playpen and Kaleb sleeping—still. She looked at the clock on the nightstand—5:00 a.m. Kaleb had gone to bed over eleven hours ago. Although he didn't understand what was going on, it was obvious exhaustion was taking its toll on them.

Kay sat up and mopped her hand across her forehead. Sweat covered her fingers. She now understood the earlier memory and the dream she'd had.

A whine from Kaleb sent her flying off the bed. She didn't want to wake up anyone in the other room. Drake and Dallas needed as much rest as they could get. It should be Drake's turn to sleep.

How can I face him? I wanted him to kiss me.

Heat scored her cheeks as she leaned over and picked up Kaleb.

And Drake didn't. He pulled away.

He was right to do that. She shouldn't develop feelings beyond friendship. Her life was out of her control, but even the little she was remembering made her wonder if it ever had been.

Put your trust in the Lord. He's in control.

Those words scrolled across her mind. Who had said that to her?

Her mother—when Kay had been trying to decide what to do after high school graduation.

Held against Kay, Kaleb wiggled and whined for a few seconds.

"No doubt you're hungry. I'll need to go into the kitchen to get you a bottle." She put her finger over her lips. "Shh. We don't want to wake up Drake."

Kaleb yawned and stretched one arm out, then cuddled against Kay.

"That's my little man." She brushed damp, dark strands of Kaleb's hair from his forehead. His skin felt warmer than usual beneath her fingertips.

She paused at the entrance into the main room and cupped her palm over his brow. He had a fever. She didn't have a thermometer, but she thought it might be a few degrees over normal.

She eased the door open and tiptoed toward the kitchen. Kaleb would need a lot of liquid to keep hydrated, and he hadn't had any for half a day. As she threw a glance toward the couch and found Drake stretched out sleeping, she held Kaleb upright, his head lying on her shoulder.

After quickly fixing a bottle with baby formula and another with water, she put them into the pockets of her sweater and hurried toward the bedroom. The jostling of her faster gait caused her son to whimper. She slowed, patting his head and holding him still. He let out a wail. Kay glanced over her shoulder, and her gaze clashed with Drake's.

He sat up, his hair tousled, his forehead crinkled. "Is everything okay?" he asked in a sleepy voice.

"Yes," Kay mumbled and disappeared into the bedroom.

But as she turned to shut the door, Drake's hand caught it, and he swung it wide. "Did you get enough rest?" He moved inside.

She tried to ignore his nearness and what it did to her heartbeat. She placed the bottles on the nightstand and sat on the bed to feed Kaleb. "Yes. I'm fine. You don't need to worry about me." *I'm a big girl, and no doubt I've dealt with rejection before.* She laid her son across her lap, cradling his head in the crook of her elbow, then picked up the bottle with formula.

Drake sank onto a chair. "I talked with Brad last night. There was a development I thought you needed to know."

"What?" Kay kept her focus on Kaleb. He

took the bottle into his mouth and began sucking on it.

"The guy who attacked you behind the café died from cyanide poisoning."

"Who poisoned him?" Kay finally looked at Drake.

"Cyanide is fast acting. No one was around him at the time of his death. He was kept in a cell by himself. No contact with other prisoners."

"Are you saying he had cyanide on him and he killed himself?"

"Not exactly. I think he took the cyanide willingly, but Brad said he didn't have it on him when he came to the jail."

"So many people have died and we have no idea why." She frowned. "Because I can't remember what happened to me."

The tension in her body must have been conveyed to Kaleb. He stopped sucking on his bottle and rolled his head away from it. She tried to entice him to drink more. Instead, his eyelids slid closed. Kay checked out how much he'd already had. Only an ounce.

"He hasn't had much. He's getting sick. I don't have a way to tell, but I believe he has a mild fever. Feel his forehead and see what you think."

Drake touched Kaleb. "You're right. I'd guess maybe a hundred or hundred and one degrees."

Kay brushed damp hair away from Kaleb's

forehead. He didn't move. "He's asleep again, and I haven't even changed his diaper. I wish I could remember if he's been sick before this."

"Maybe it's teething. My sister used to complain about how grumpy her son got when he was getting a tooth."

"I guess that's a possibility, even if I couldn't feel any coming in. I'll keep an eye on him. He needs more liquid, but I'll let him sleep a little longer. That is, if he doesn't wake up when I change his diaper."

"Isn't there an adage that says never wake a sleeping baby?"

She shrugged. "Beats me, but if he becomes dehydrated, we'll have to take him into the hospital or the very least to see a doctor."

"And that wouldn't be safe for y'all."

"Stress can affect how healthy a person is, and what Kaleb's gone through this week certainly has been stressful. I'm going to try to make his life as normal as possible." Kay laid her son in the middle of the bed, then retrieved what she needed to change his diaper. She'd thought he would wake up, but he didn't. "Well, I guess I'll put him back in the playpen with Mr. Teddy, but only for an hour. Then I'll try giving him some more formula or water."

When Kaleb was settled again cuddling next to his stuffed animal, Kay slowly backed out of the room. She needed to tell Drake about her dream and what she remembered about her previous life.

But when the front door opened and Dallas poked his head into the cabin, saying the El Paso office wanted to talk to Drake, he shrugged into his coat and decided to trade places with his partner ten minutes early.

As Drake left the cabin and Dallas came inside, Kay took one look at his slumping shoulders and tired eyes and said, "I'm up for the day. Why don't you use the bed? It's gotta be more comfortable than the couch. Kaleb is still sleeping, but I'd like to move him out into the main room. Unless you want something to eat first."

"Nope. Rest over food. Guard duty is exhausting. Do you want to bring the playpen out here?"

"Yes." Kay crossed to the bedroom. "Will you help me?"

"Sure."

"What does El Paso want?" Kay took hold of one end of the playpen while Dallas lifted the other.

"Just some chatter about the human trafficking case he's working on. Nothing new on yours. Still no identification of the three dead men."

"What if they're not from the United States? Especially since this area is so close to the southern border."

"It takes longer, but we're checking abroad, too, especially with the Mexican authorities." After putting the playpen near the couch, Dallas walked toward the bedroom. "Don't let me oversleep."

"I won't."

"Good night."

When Dallas left, Kay touched the locket around her neck, opening it and staring at the two photos in it. She had to be Kaleb's mother or someone very close to him. Suddenly she had a vision of holding Kaleb, tears running down her face, ones that wouldn't stop. Grief engulfed her, her sobs echoing through her mind. Someone she'd loved had died recently. Who? Her husband?

She looked at her ring finger as if to reconfirm there was no evidence she'd worn a wedding ring on her tanned left hand. New tears ran down her cheeks. She couldn't shake the feeling that part of her had died. Her chest constricted, making breathing difficult.

She didn't want to remember if it was going to be this painful.

She stared at Kaleb sleeping, his hair damp. She grazed her fingers over his face. He didn't feel any hotter. He rooted around, touched Mr. Teddy and snuggled closer to it.

She couldn't lose him.

* * *

When Dallas relieved him next, Drake strode toward the cabin, eager to see Kay. He'd hated leaving her earlier. All he could think about while outside was her and Kaleb. He went over every minute of the time they had been together. At first he'd told himself it was because he needed to figure out who was after her, but by the end of his shift, he couldn't deny his growing feelings for her.

As he entered the cabin, his gaze immediately found Kay sitting on the couch, giving Kaleb a bottle of baby formula. The sight took his breath away.

She looked up at him.

For a moment neither of them moved. Then she dropped her head, breaking their visual connection.

"How's he doing?"

"Sleeping a lot. Drinking a little. I checked his mouth earlier, and he does have a tooth coming in."

"Well, then that's probably why he's fussy and has a slight fever." He closed the space between them and sank down on the couch near her. "Is he still sweating?"

"Yes, that's why I haven't put any logs on the fire." When Kaleb stopped sucking, Kay put the bottle on the end table and held the baby against her shoulder while patting his back. "I didn't have a chance to tell you earlier about the dream I had. The past hour I've been sitting here thinking about it."

"What dream?"

"About the fire I was caught in. I dreamed some more about it and realized why I was there. I'm a firefighter. I was in the house searching for a little girl. I found her and got her outside alive."

"Where?"

She shook her head. "That I don't know, but knowing what I did for a living might help you find out who I am."

"Yes, but now that we know someone is after you, I'm not sure about alerting anyone that you're alive and here. I'll call El Paso and have them deal with this as quietly as possible. First, they can check to see if any women firefighters have been reported missing."

"If we know who I am, that might help me remember more. I've also had this overwhelming feeling of grief."

"Someone you cared about died?"

"Yes, or I feel this way because of the situation I'm in. Not knowing who you are is a kind of death."

"Every day you're remembering bits and pieces. It'll all come together." He prayed it did, because something had happened to cause three men to come after her and end up dying in the attempt.

Kay rose and put a sleeping Kaleb into the playpen. "I need coffee. Do you want some?"

"I'll get it." Drake prepared two mugs and brought them into the living room. "Have you been up the whole time I was outside?"

"Yes. Can't stop thinking about what I'm remembering."

"About being a firefighter?" Why hadn't she been reported missing? If she'd taken vacation days over Thanksgiving, she should have been back to work by now. But more important, who was she grieving? Had she witnessed something that led to the sorrow but also the people after her?

"No. I've been trying to recall any additional information about who I am. I get close, then my thoughts shut down. It's like I'm standing in front of a creepy old house and being taunted to go inside, but every time I take a step closer, a cold wind sweeps over me and I freeze in place."

Drake panned the room for something to take her mind off her situation. He spied a stack of board games in a bookcase. "Tell you what. I'm going to call El Paso and get them working on what you've told me, then let's play a game. There's Monopoly, Clue and Scrabble."

He covered her hand for a few seconds, then stood. "Your choice."

Drake shrugged into his coat and headed outside to get the sat phone from Dallas. But there wasn't a sign of him anywhere. Probably out back.

Drake circled the cabin. Still no Dallas. The hairs on his nape tingled and goose bumps streaked down his arms.

The side door to the detached storage shed where they kept their vehicle was ajar. He crept toward the building, his gun raised. As he entered, the door creaked, alerting anyone inside he was coming in.

Out of the corner of his eye, a movement on the other side of his vehicle caught his attention. He swiveled toward it.

ELEVEN

Kay looked out the window over the sink. Fifteen minutes had passed since Drake left. She'd thought he would be back by now. But he wasn't out front. She refilled their mugs and set them on the end table, then went around the cabin checking out each of the windows.

Drake and Dallas were gone.

She rubbed her sweaty palms on her jeans. Maybe she'd just missed them as they rounded a side. She hurried and retraced her steps, inspecting outside then pulling the blinds closed. Her heartbeat increased with each sight of vacant landscape.

She glanced at Kaleb, still sleeping in the playpen, then at the front door. What should she do?

Lock the door. Find a weapon.

She quickly did both. Drake had left a gun inside. She grabbed it, recalling the last time she'd held a weapon. She'd wounded a man who had attacked them at the ranch. To protect Kaleb, she would again. But her hand holding the pistol shook.

The knob on the front door rattled. She kept her gaze fixed on the entrance but sidestepped to perch behind the kitchen counter. Then she lifted the gun, using both hands to steady her aim.

Sweat beaded her forehead and rolled down her face. She prepared herself for the door to burst open, but instead the sound of a key being inserted into the lock resonated through the air. She began to relax until she realized anyone after her could have taken the key off Drake or Dallas.

The door slowly opened.

Kay stiffened.

"Kay, it's Drake."

Relief nearly sent her to the floor. She grasped the edge of the counter and clung to it to keep herself upright.

Drake entered and glanced around until he spotted her. "Is something wrong? You locked the door."

"When you didn't come back after fifteen minutes, I got worried. I checked out each window and couldn't see you or Dallas anywhere. I thought about going outside looking for you, but I was afraid someone had overpowered you two. I locked the door and grabbed your spare gun." She held it up, then put it down on the counter.

She might know how to use it, but she didn't like holding one—or shooting one.

Drake shut the door and locked it, as was his protocol every time one of them was outside on guard duty. "I'm sorry. I should have locked it even when I went out briefly. When I couldn't find Dallas—I searched everywhere. He was in the shed looking out the window that faces away from the cabin toward the nearby hills. He spotted two teenagers, probably no more than fourteen or fifteen, riding dune buggies. But he didn't know it until they came closer. He called his cousin and discovered that they're his neighbor's sons. Thankfully they didn't stay long." He grinned. "Then I had to call the office in El Paso."

"Any news there?"

"They have a name of one of the men who attacked us at the ranch. Jose Lopez. The Mexican authorities said he works for the *Muerte* Cartel in northern Mexico."

"The death cartel! I don't even remember being in Mexico in years." The second she said the last sentence she realized how ridiculous that statement was.

"They have ties in the United States. Drugs aren't the only thing they traffic."

Kay made her way to the couch. She needed to sit. "Who runs that cartel?"

"They are relatively new on the scene but expanding rapidly. They are relentless and merciless. They have a lot of money behind them. Not as much is known about them as some of the other cartels. There's a public face to it but also a private one. Diego Redondo is the public face. He lives in Juárez."

The name Diego Redondo meant nothing to her. How might she have angered him? "But you think someone else really runs it?"

"Yes. When we don't know everyone involved at the top, it makes it more difficult to bring the organization down." Finally, Drake took a seat next to her. "On a good note, I think the information you gave me will help the El Paso office track you down—quietly. I stressed that."

"Obviously, the wrong people already know the area I'm in. I just wish I knew why they're after me. I'm not a drug user or I would have been a basket case by now. I don't care if I can't remember a lot of my past. I wouldn't be a dealer. My father died from a drug reaction when he was in the hosp…" Her eyes widened.

The corners of his mouth tilted upward. "If we talk enough, no telling what you'll recall."

She searched her mind for memories to support her statement. She found snippets of her childhood that confirmed its truth—visiting an older man hooked up to monitors in the hospital, hugging her mother while she sobbed at a funeral, flipping out when she discovered her boyfriend in high school taking a prescription drug he got from a classmate. "I'm glad I'm remembering parts of my life, but what I need to know is what happened to me these past couple of weeks. Why did I end up in Big Bend with Kaleb?" She turned toward Drake and sat cross-legged on the couch so she could face him. "I've learned a few things so far about myself. I'm impatient, or at least with this I am."

He chuckled. "I'll tell you a secret. I would be, too. Most people who have amnesia aren't running for their life." He took her hand, cupping it between both of his. "I'm impressed at how well you're holding up."

She became lost in the bright blue of his eyes. It reminded her of a time as a teenager when she'd swum in a beautiful blue mountain lake. She could fall in love with this guy so easily. But all of what was happening to her seemed surreal. No relationship should be built on shaky ground, and after hearing about the *Muerte* Cartel, she didn't know that she would walk away from this situation.

"You're tensing." He clasped her other hand and bowed his head. "Lord, we need Your protection. Show us what to do."

"Please keep us safe and help us to get to the bottom of what's going on," Kay added.

Drake's stomach rumbled.

Kay looked at him and laughed. "I think someone in this room is hungry." She slipped her hands from his grasp and rose. "The least I can do is fix you something to eat. Another thing I'm discovering is I know my way around the kitchen. Eggs or oatmeal?"

"I'll take both. I've worked up quite an appetite. That's what fear can do for you—at least for me."

"You, afraid?" He always seemed confident and in control.

"Sure. That's what helps me stay alive."

"Good to know. I've certainly had my share of fear lately." Kay smiled at him as she stepped into the kitchen. "I'll see what I can whip up for you with our limited supplies."

Drake pushed to his feet. "I'm going to wash up."

Instead of heading for the one bathroom in the cabin, he stopped next to the playpen and leaned over to brush his fingertips along the curve of Kaleb's face. "His skin is moist and cool."

She imagined the soft feel of his touch along her face. The thought sent a shiver through her body. She quickly turned her effort to making breakfast before the morning slipped into afternoon.

* * *

As Drake came around the side of the cabin from the back, the sat phone rang. He answered the call from the Texas Rangers' office in El Paso. "Tell me you have good news."

"We found her. Her name is Kayden Rollins, and she's a firefighter in Albuquerque, New Mexico. The department reported her missing yesterday. She'd been on vacation but didn't show up for work when she should have. She didn't call to let the station know she wasn't coming in, so they checked on her. Right before she left, she told one of the firefighters that she was concerned about driving down to see her sister in Mexico. The sister lives not too far from Juárez. Kayden's house was ransacked. They reported it to the police. That's all I know at this time, but the detective working the case will stay in touch with us."

"What did you tell him about why we were inquiring about Kay?"

"That I wasn't at liberty to say anything. I got the description of her car and license plate number. I told him we'd be on the lookout for her and her car. I'm sending you a copy of a photo the police had of Kayden Rollins."

Drake waited until the picture appeared on his phone. He stared at the smile that dimpled Kay's cheeks. Her dark eyes gleamed, and her long light brown hair was pulled back in a pony-tail. None of the fear and weariness he'd seen was evident in the photo. He wanted to see her like that.

"Kay is Kayden Rollins. Give me the description of the car and her tag number. She's remembering more each day."

After Texas Ranger Pierce recited the license plate information, he said, "It's a gray 2011 Taurus."

"Thanks. I'll try to pull up a picture of one to see if it jogs her memory. Can you have the detective send you a photo of the outside of her home? That might help, too." Although Pierce didn't mention anyone living with Kay—no, Kayden—Drake asked, "Does she live alone?"

"Yes."

"No child, husband, boyfriend?"

"I figured you'd want to know, and I asked. No one. She lives in the home she grew up in. Her mother died a few years ago and left the place to Kayden and her sister, Kassandra."

"See if you can find out the location of her sister in Mexico. Did Kay cross the border at Juárez? Also, check the Presidio and Del Rio crossings and the recently reopened one at Boquillas."

"I'll see what I can find out about her going and returning and let you know."

The cabin's door opened. Drake turned and waved to Dallas. "And I'll talk to Kay—den." Maybe she went by Kay and that was why she'd responded to his suggestion to use it. After he ended the call, he handed the sat phone to Dallas. "Pierce might call back with more information." Drake gave his partner a rundown on what Pierce had discovered about Kay.

Dallas pocketed the phone. "She was visiting her sister in Mexico?"

"Yeah. Do you think Kaleb is her sister's child?"

"Maybe, but why would she have the baby? Where is her sister?"

"Pierce is checking that out. I feel for the first time we have some useful information that may lead to what's going on."

Drake started for the cabin. Dallas had only voiced two of the many questions Drake had. If Kay had visited Mexico, it could explain why she'd ended up in Big Bend. It was on the border, but then, how did she return to the United States? There were two legal border crossings that were closer to Big Bend than the one at Juárez. Of course, it was possible if Kay was fleeing the people after her that she crossed the Mexican border somewhere along the hundred-plus miles that the national park encompassed. Or at Boquillas, a small crossing used by people who visited Big Bend to go to Mexico for a few hours. She wouldn't want to cross where someone would be expecting her to.

When Drake went inside, he found Kay holding Kaleb, pacing from one end of the living room to the other. Would he ever get the answers to what happened? Some people never remembered, especially if a traumatic incident caused the amnesia.

"How's Kaleb?"

"Settling down. He finally drank almost two ounces. I wonder if he's coming down with a cold. He was breathing heavily while sucking his bottle."

Drake stroked Kaleb's head. "It looks like he's sleeping now."

"I tried to lay him down ten minutes ago, but he woke up and started crying. Pacing was the only way to calm him down." She walked to the playpen and gently placed him on the mat and covered him with a blanket. When she straightened, she watched Kaleb sleeping. "This has been so hard on him. We've got to get to the bottom of what's going on."

Drake clasped her shoulders and kneaded his hands into her tight knots. "It's been harder on you. Thankfully he doesn't know everything that's gone down."

"And it has to stay that way."

He turned her around. "We need to talk."

"What's happened?"

"I talked to Pierce at the El Paso office, and with the information about you being a firefighter, he was able to track down where you live and your name."

Kay didn't say anything but stepped over to the couch and sank onto it. "From your serious look, I figure it's not good news." Straightening her shoulders, she sucked in a deep breath. "Okay, tell me."

Drake relaxed his own tense muscles and sat next to Kay. "Sorry about that. A lot of questions have been answered, but not all of them. You work for the fire department in Albuquerque. When you didn't show up for work and didn't call in, they became worried. They went by to see if you were okay and called the police after they saw your house had been ransacked and you weren't there."

"So someone came into my house and I managed to flee with Kaleb? Why did I end up in Big Bend?"

"According to your coworkers, you don't have a child. You were on vacation over Thanksgiving and driving to your sister's. She lives somewhere southeast of Juárez."

Her eyes grew wide. "I have a sister who lives in Mexico?" She glanced back at the playpen.

"Then where did I get Kaleb? How did I end up in the park?" She lowered her head and scrubbed her fingertips into her forehead as though somehow that would lift the barrier to her memories.

He wanted to pull her against him. He couldn't even imagine how hard it was to have important parts of the past left blank. His heart ached for her.

When she looked up at him, tears glistened in her eyes. She clutched her necklace, opening the locket. "How did I end up with photos of myself and Kaleb in this?"

"What if Kaleb is your nephew? You could easily have a picture of him."

"Then where are my sister and Kaleb's father?"

"The El Paso office is looking into that." He knew Kay felt helpless, had since he'd found her, but so did he. He wanted to take this all away for her, but he didn't even know: Away from what?

"Meanwhile, what do we do?"

"We stay here. Can you remember anything about your sister? Who she married? Your coworkers told the police her name is Kassandra and your real name is Kayden Rollins."

"Kayden? Kassandra…" Kay leaped to her feet. "Excuse me."

Drake rose. He didn't think her eyes could get

any wider, but they did. Her color washed from her face and her hands shook.

She whirled around and rushed toward the bathroom. She slammed the door. The click of the lock reverberated through the living room.

Drake moved to the playpen to make sure Kaleb was still asleep. He'd handled this all wrong and didn't know what to do. Ever since he'd realized his emotions were tied up in this case, he'd felt as though he was a juggler who had lost all his tossed balls.

Dallas opened the front door and stuck his head into the cabin. "A call from El Paso for you."

Drake hurried across the room, hoping this was good news.

Shaking all over, Kay sank down onto the lip of the bathtub.

I have a sister. Kassandra. Why haven't I remembered that? I've had memories about my father and mother.

She closed her eyes and tried to picture her sister. Was she older or younger? Was Kaleb Kassandra's baby?

No image materialized in her mind.

She took in one deep breath after another to compose herself. She needed to remain calm and figure out what was going on. But that was easier said than done.

I feel so lost, God. What do I do now?

Silence greeted her desperate plea.

She squeezed her hands into fists until her fingernails dug into her palms. She relaxed her tight grip and rose. Sitting in the bathroom wasn't going to help her to fill the blank spaces in her mind. As she started for the exit, a soft rap sounded against the door.

"Kay, are you all right?"

"Yes, I'm fine," she said with more forceful confidence than she felt.

"I have more news."

"I'll be out in a second." Kay—or should she refer to herself as Kayden?—glanced at her image in the mirror. She looked as though she'd been put through the wringer. After she splashed cold water on her face, she left the bathroom.

Drake waited for her, lounging against the rear of the couch, his feet and arms crossed. "I know this is a lot to take in all at once."

"What else did you find out?"

"You drove into Mexico via the El Paso border crossing the day before Thanksgiving. There's no record of you returning to the US. Your sister is married to Alejandro Soto, a wealthy Mexican businessman who has several residences. Their wedding took place in Albuquerque two years ago. The El Paso office will continue looking for information on your sister and Senor Soto."

"Has anyone contacted them?"

"No one was at their main house near Juárez. The Mexican authorities are searching for them."

Her sister lived in Mexico? How did she meet Alejandro Soto? She'd been remembering earlier events in her life, so why didn't she recall her sister's marriage to Alejandro? That should be a wonderful memory. "What if I was supposed to look after Kaleb while they went on a vacation? That would explain why he was with me and not them."

"That's possible. This is when we have to be patient and let the police here and in Mexico do their job." He chuckled. "Now I'll just have to find a way to follow my own advice. I'm usually in the field running down clues and answers."

"Waiting isn't easy. Sitting around waiting can drain more energy than hiking in Big Bend."

Drake pushed off the couch and approached her. He cradled her face and grazed his thumbs across her cheeks under her eyes. "You look exhausted. I'll watch Kaleb while you take a nap in the bedroom."

The feel of his hands—a mixture of sensations from warmth to a rough texture—on her skin threw her off kilter. Her legs threatened to buckle. She clutched his arms and steadied herself. She was more tired than she'd realized. It was as though the past few days were finally catching up with her.

"Okay. But you'll have to go back outside in three hours. You'll need to rest, too."

"I don't think I can. I figure Pierce from the El Paso office will call me with updates. If Kaleb gets up, I can change his diaper and give him something to drink or eat. I'm not a total novice around babies."

"I've noticed, and Kaleb responds to you."

He inched closer until his warm breath caressed her cheek. The intensity in his eyes held her captive. She couldn't move if she wanted to. All she wanted to do was draw him even closer.

He dipped his head and brushed his lips across hers. Chills flashed through her body as his arms encircled her and brought her against him. She clung to Drake as if he were her lifeline, and in many ways, he was. She probably would have died if he hadn't found her, especially now that she knew men had been looking for her in Big Bend.

When Drake lifted his head, his arms remained locked about her. The sense of strength and safety in his embrace shored up her flailing emotions. When he released her and stepped away, she missed his nearness.

"Wake me up in an hour. If I sleep any longer, I'll never get any sleep later."

"I will."

The cherished feelings produced by his smile fluttered through her as she moved toward the bedroom. After that kiss, she didn't know if she could get any rest. All her senses felt charged.

And when she lay down on the bed, her mind swirled with random thoughts. She was falling for Drake, but how could that be real? She didn't know who she was beyond the little she'd learned. There was so much more she needed to know.

She tried to relax, but questions inundated her. What if the people after her had done something to her sister and her husband? What would make her flee with Kaleb? Why couldn't she remember unless it was bad? She couldn't picture Kassandra or Alejandro, but her worry grew. It was just her and Kaleb right now.

Advice from her mother filled her mind. *You can't let worry dictate what you're going to do. God is in control. Give your worry to Him.*

Wise words but hard to follow. She closed her eyes and willed all thoughts from her. She fixated on the feelings Drake generated in her when he kissed her, and soon she drifted off…

A sound disturbed her peace. She barely lifted

her eyelids when a bright light jerked her totally from sleep.

Drake stood in the entrance, cradling Kaleb against him.

Kay struggled to sit up, cobwebs still clinging to her mind. "It's been an hour?"

"No. But something is wrong. Kaleb is burning up."

TWELVE

"Kaleb woke up two times, crying and drawing up his legs. The first time before I could pick him up, he settled down a little. I patted him, and he went back to sleep. This second time when I picked him up, he felt hotter than before, and he's breathing rapidly." Drake passed the baby to Kay.

She laid him on the bed and put her palm against his forehead. "You're right. His temperature is going up. I haven't had to change his diaper in several hours. Did you?"

"No."

Kay unsnapped Kaleb's onesie and opened his diaper. Her hand shaking, she stared at him. "He's bloated, and his stool is runny."

"And he's pale." Drake lifted his tiny hand and held it between his. "This is cold and clammy. I think he's going into shock. I'm calling for help."

While Kay changed Kaleb's diaper, Drake

hurried outside to get the sat phone from Dallas. "Kaleb's sick. We need to take him to the hospital."

"That's almost two hours away."

"Yeah, that's why I'm calling El Paso. He can be airlifted to the hospital. I could take him and you could stay here with Kay." Drake punched in the numbers for the El Paso office, quickly listing the baby's symptoms to Pierce.

"I'll get a helicopter to bring him to the hospital as well as talk to a doctor to see what you need to do. I'll call you back and let you know the ETA."

Drake disconnected the call and started back to the cabin.

Dallas followed. "She'll never go for you taking Kaleb without her."

"I know. But I'm going to suggest that option. It would be safer for her."

"Even if she isn't his mother, she loves that little fella. At least in El Paso, we'll have more manpower to guard her and Kaleb." Dallas stopped on the porch. "If you need me, I'll be right out here."

"Yeah, we still need to be vigilant. I'll let you know when the helicopter is going to arrive." Drake ducked inside.

Kay stood in the middle of the living room, holding Kaleb, tears running down her face. "I knew he wasn't feeling well, but…" She swallowed hard. "At first I thought he was teething and then maybe he was getting a cold or exhausted and confused from all that's been happening. I should have…"

Drake closed the space between them. "This developed quickly. We're dealing with a lot." The sat phone rang, and he answered the call from Pierce. "When will the helicopter be here?"

"Forty-five minutes. The doctor thinks he definitely needs to go the hospital. It could be several serious illnesses. If he's going into shock, keep him calm, warm and comfortable. Keep checking his pulse and breathing. He could be dehydrated. If he hasn't had a lot of fluids, try to get him to take some. In the meantime, I'm working on security at the hospital."

"Anything else about the case?" He didn't want to take Kay and Kaleb away from the safe house, but he'd seen a person rapidly decline and die.

"Yes. Since I talked with you, we discovered Alejandro Soto has done business with Diego Redondo, who is the known head of the *Muerte* Cartel."

"What kind of business?"

"Legit, as far as we can tell."

"Could Soto be secretly connected to the cartel?"

"Maybe. The authorities don't know everyone involved in the running of this new cartel."

"Is Soto still missing?"

"Yes, as well as his wife and child who might be Kaleb. So, you see why it's important to secure Kayden Rollins."

Drake turned away from Kay and headed into the kitchen. "He might not be part of the cartel—maybe he crossed someone in it. What if something happened to her sister and Soto? Kay might be a witness to it and somehow managed to escape with their baby. Do you have a picture of them?"

"I'm working on that. As soon as I do, I'll send it to your phone."

"Let me know any updates you get."

"Will do."

Drake ended the call and returned to the living room.

"Who's missing?" Kay asked as she cuddled Kaleb and paced behind the couch, the baby crying the whole time.

"So far, the authorities can't find your sister or her husband."

She stopped pacing. What color Kay had left in her face drained from it. "You think they're dead?"

"I don't know what happened, and right now you need to focus on Kaleb. Pierce talked with a doctor." Drake repeated what the El Paso Texas Ranger had said.

"He could be dehydrated, especially after what occurred in Big Bend. Anna and I were giving him fluids, as much as he would take, but in the past day or so, he hasn't drunk what he should if he was still dehydrated from the park."

"Don't beat yourself up over this. When he left the hospital in Cactus Grove, he was hydrated or the doctor wouldn't have let him go."

"I took him before he was dismissed."

"But the doctor was going to let him leave when he stopped by at the end of the day. Kaleb had been taken off the IV fluids." Drake made his way into the kitchen. "Check his pulse and breathing. I'll fix a bottle."

He'd known Kay and Kaleb less than a week, but they had already become very important to him beyond being a case he was working on. He'd kissed her—twice—and he shouldn't have. He'd gone against what he'd decided earlier: strictly a professional relationship. He'd never mixed his professional and private lives. He might now have Kay's real name, but he didn't really know her. He couldn't lose his focus. Two crying children in the back seat of the truck Shanna had stopped distracted her, giving the driver enough time to draw a gun and kill her. He'd made a promise to protect Kay and Kaleb, and he would. There was no room for anything else.

* * *

Kay stared out the hospital window at the darkness interrupted by the lights of El Paso. She chewed on her thumbnail and waited. Drake had left a few minutes ago to coordinate with Texas Ranger Pierce concerning the security. In the meantime, Dallas and an El Paso police officer guarded the room.

She wished Drake was here. Not that they talked much when he was, but his presence had a calming effect on her. She needed that, especially now. On the helicopter ride to Mercy Hospital, it broke her heart each time Kaleb screamed.

His intestine was blocked. The bowel obstruction was severe enough that he had to be operated on to correct it. If they had waited too much longer, Kaleb's chances of recovery would have decreased, and he would have irreversible damage to his intestine. She still didn't know if that wouldn't be the outcome.

The door opened, and she pivoted toward it, hoping it was the doctor with good news. It wasn't, but Drake had returned, a sober expression on his face. Since the cabin he'd been distant, as though they hadn't shared a kiss. She'd missed that caring, concerned man, but he had a job to do. Her life and Kaleb's depended on him doing it.

"Did the doctor come in yet?" he asked as he bridged the distance between them.

"No."

He shut the blinds. "I don't want you standing in the window."

"We're on the fifth floor."

"The cartel has access to snipers, and we need to take precautions with that in mind." Drake's voice almost sounded cold.

"If you meant to scare me, you have." She sat in a chair away from the window. "I was going stir-crazy waiting for the surgeon to let me know how Kaleb is doing."

His features softened. "I'm sorry. I know you're scared. Although there aren't any tall buildings nearby, a sniper can fire from a location a mile away."

"How's security here?"

"It's coming together quickly, but as soon as it's safe to transport Kaleb to a more secure place to recover, we will. I'll feel a lot better when we can." He took a chair across from her. "I have photos of both Kassandra and her husband. I need you to look at them. They might trigger your memory." He withdrew a cell phone and clicked it on.

She was almost afraid to see the pictures. She needed to recall, but there was part of her that didn't want to. She was afraid of what she would remember. Drawing in a calming breath, she reached for the phone.

"Kassandra is your—"

A knock interrupted his words. She gasped, dropped her arm and swiveled toward the entrance while Drake rose, pocketed his cell and went to open the door. He stepped to the side to allow the surgeon, Dr. Santos, inside.

Kay stood, preparing herself for what he might tell her.

There was no indication from his look until he took several steps into the room. A smile slowly transformed his solemn expression. "The surgery was successful. We were able to repair the damage, and he should make a full recovery."

"Oh, good," Kay said on a long breath.

"When's the earliest we can remove him from the hospital?" Drake asked the surgeon.

"Kaleb needs to have IV feedings until he can eat normally and his bowels work properly. We need to make sure the intussusception doesn't return."

"Then he'll stay until you release him." Kay shot Drake a look meant to silence any objections. She needed to make sure Kaleb would recover fully. What if her taking him away from the hospital in Cactus Grove before he was officially released had in some way caused his intussusception? She wasn't taking any chances this time.

Dr. Santos put his hand on the doorknob. "Kaleb will return to this room shortly."

When the surgeon left, Kay steeled herself for Drake's argument about the danger she and Kaleb were in if they stayed in such a public place for any length of time. She understood where he was coming from, but she would make sure Kaleb stayed until he was well. She couldn't lose him.

"What about the people after you?"

There was no anger in Drake's voice, only inquiry. "He may not be my child, but he's most likely my nephew. I'll protect him with my life if I have to." An image of her running away from a large hacienda in the middle of the night with Kaleb pressed against her chest invaded her mind.

I might have a few hours before he knows I'm gone.

Who was *he*? What had made her flee with Kaleb in the dark? She sank onto the chair, trying to force the memory to answer those questions. The desert air at night was chilly. Did she grab enough to keep her and Kaleb warm?

"Kay. Kayden. What's wrong?"

She blinked and focused on Drake's face looming before her. He knelt in front of her, worry deepening the lines on his tanned face. "I had a memory of fleeing with Kaleb—" she shook her head "—but nothing that would help."

"I'll put Kaleb's safety first, but in the end, that might mean leaving here. That doesn't mean I wouldn't get medical help for him. If I say we must leave, will you trust me?"

He'd done everything he could to keep her alive, and she knew in the future he would. She nodded.

"Tell me about the memory. You never know what will be a clue to help us."

She described what she remembered. "I keep trying to recall what I did next. I can't."

"I'm more concerned with what happened before you ran away." He withdrew his cell phone and handed it to her. "That's a picture of your sister."

Kay stared at an image of herself with longer hair. "We're twins. I should have known that." She clasped the locket about her neck. "The photo isn't me but Kassandra." She closed her eyes, willing herself to recall anything.

Nothing.

"Sorry, I wish I could help more. Do you have a picture of her husband?"

Drake slid his finger across the screen, bringing up a photo of a tall, handsome guy with black hair. He was dressed in a dark business suit with a red tie—the color of blood. "Do you remember anything about him?"

Kay couldn't take her eyes off the tie. An image of a man lying in a pool of blood suddenly filled her mind. But the dead body wasn't Kassandra's husband. "No…nothing concrete."

"Did you have a memory right now?"

She nodded. "An older man dead on a floor. I don't know where, and I don't know who he is or how he ended up there. It might not even be real." She hoped it wasn't.

"Can you describe him?"

"Stocky build, deeply tanned face, short black hair."

"If I got a sketch artist here, do you think you could work with him to come up with a picture of the man?"

"I'll try anything to help put an end to this mess. Do you think I witnessed a murder and that is why I'm on the run? If so, why would I take Kaleb from his home?"

"I don't know. The more we discover, the more questions we have. The Mexican authorities are still searching for your sister and her husband."

"Could it have been an attempt at kidnapping Kaleb?"

"That's a possibility." Drake rose. "Right now your focus needs to be on Kaleb. He's going to be all right. You heard the surgeon. We got him here in time."

What if Kaleb had died before he could get help, all because someone was after them? This madness had to stop. *God, help us figure out what's going on before it's too late.*

Dallas entered the hospital room and held the door open while a nurse wheeled in Kaleb, hooked up to monitors and an IV. His eyes were closed, but he looked peaceful, nothing like the helicopter ride to the hospital. He'd cried most of the trip, creating a knot in her stomach that still hadn't unraveled.

While Dallas and Drake conversed quietly, Kay approached the nurse. "What can I do to help him?"

"Be here when he wakes up. Seeing a familiar face will reassure him. If there's a problem, use this call button." The young woman pointed to its location. "As the medication wears off, he'll become more alert. We'll be in and out to check on him."

"Thank you." When the nurse left, Kay brushed his hair away from his face, wanting to hold Kaleb so much.

Dallas soon followed the nurse from the room, and Drake joined Kay at the bedside. "Still nothing on the location of your sister and brother-in-law."

Brother-in-law made it sound like she had a close relationship with Kassandra's husband, but she couldn't remember anything—not even what he looked like if Drake hadn't shown his picture to her.

"Why don't you try to rest? I'll be here if he wakes up, but he probably won't for a while."

Kay glanced at the lounge chair and shook her head. "I don't think I can sleep."

"Try. Dallas is calling the office about getting a sketch artist over here. It might help to figure out who you saw dead." He clasped her shoulders. "You're tense. Relax, at least. We're making progress."

"Progress? I still can't remember, and someone is still out there looking for us."

"But we know who you are, who you went to visit and mostly likely who Kaleb's parents are. A day ago we didn't."

She sighed. "I'll try. No guarantees."

Kay put her feet up and leaned the lounge chair back as far as it would go. Drake gave her a pillow and put a light blanket over her. He bent over and kissed her forehead. "I'll be here. I won't let anyone hurt you or Kaleb."

His reassuring words burrowed deep into her thoughts, and slowly the tension that held her in a viselike grip loosened. She closed her eyes and surrendered to the darkness…

Strong, large hands squeezed so tightly she gasped for air, but none filled her lungs. Shoved back against the wall, his grip making the blackness swirl, she had to open her eyes—to see who was trying to kill her—but her lids remained anchored down. She wanted to scream, fight, but she couldn't move.

From somewhere deep down, she forced herself to look at the killer. When her eyes bolted open, a scream escaped her.

Bright lights flooded the hospital room.

She blinked.

Drake's face loomed in front of her.

"I—I know who killed my sister."

THIRTEEN

Kay trembled so badly she struggled with the lever to the lounge chair's footrest before she finally managed to put it down. The pain on her face tore at his composure.

Drake knelt next to her, clasping her hand. "You saw your sister being murdered?"

She nodded.

When she didn't say anything else, he asked, "Who?"

For a long moment, she stared off into space as though she were reliving the incident all over again. Her breathing shortened. Her eyes dilated.

"Kay?" He rose and perched on the chair's arm.

"Her husband choked her to death." The words came out in a halting, husky voice.

He'd wanted her to remember because without those memories she would always feel incomplete—much like the disappearance of his sister.

With Beth, there was no closure, but he hoped Kay could have some when this was all over.

He embraced her and held her against his side. "What happened?" He hated asking her to relive it yet again, but her life and Kaleb's were in danger, and he needed to figure out what was going on and why.

"The nightmare I've been having about being strangled was really what happened to Kassandra. I got a look at the person with his hands around my—no, her neck. He was wearing a gold ring with a crest on it. When he let go—" she choked on the phrase and cleared her throat "—she slumped to the floor. I escaped her bedroom with the backpack I found in Big Bend. I'd been hiding in Kaleb's room, which was connected to hers."

"What made you hide?"

She lowered her head and shook it. "I don't know."

"Do you remember what you did next?"

"As soon as he left her bedroom, I checked Kassandra…" Her breath caught on the last word.

Drake waited for Kay to continue. She lifted her tear-filled eyes to his.

A crashing sound in the corridor caused Kay to jerk back, her attention flying to the door.

He dragged her gaze back to him. "What else did you do?"

"I grabbed Kaleb from his room. Then I carried out the plan I'd promised Kassandra I would do."

"What plan?"

"Flee with Kaleb to the United States. My sister had a car stashed away for the escape. She knew she couldn't cross the border anywhere near El Paso because her husband would know. Kassandra was frightened of Alejandro. She couldn't stay with him any longer. He was supposed to be at a big meeting until evening. He came home early."

"Why was she afraid?"

"She wouldn't tell me much. She wanted to wait until we were safe." She swiped her hand across her cheeks. "We always shared everything, but all she would say is that he was abusive and she couldn't stay any longer. She feared for Kaleb, too. I figured once I got her away from the house I'd find out what he did to make her so afraid. Near the border the car broke down, and I had to walk the rest of the way. I avoided anyone who might be working for Alejandro, which was everyone I saw.

A soft rap sounded on the door a few seconds before it opened. Drake rose and faced the nurse who came into the room.

The woman exchanged the IV fluid bag with a new one, checked the monitors, then wrote on Kaleb's chart. "His vital signs are good." She smiled as she headed to the door and left.

Kay glanced at the clock on the wall. "I can't believe I slept two hours. You've got to be tired, too."

"I'll rest later. Right now, I need to talk to Pierce about what you've remembered. He's been working with the Mexican authorities. He's with the man in charge of hospital security. I'll send Dallas in to keep you company." He also wanted to walk through the hospital and see if there was anything else they needed to do to keep Kay and Kaleb safe.

"You don't have to do that. Knowing Dallas and a police officer are outside the door is enough."

He opened his mouth to protest.

She held up a palm. "I want to be alone. I have so much going on in my head. I need quiet time to make sense of what has been going on."

"Okay. I shouldn't be gone more than an hour. You have my cell phone number. Call if you need me."

"I will."

He paused at the door and glanced at her. "Do you want me to bring you coffee?"

She nodded.

Drake stepped out into the hallway and told Dallas what he was going to do, then headed for the first-floor security office. He took the stairs, needing to do something physical. He'd delved deeply to keep calm as Kay told him about the dream and who she thought killed her sister. All he'd wanted to do was make sure Soto paid for his crimes. If the man could kill his own wife, then it would mean nothing to him to murder Kay. No wonder she'd tried to forget what she'd witnessed. No wonder she'd thought she was being strangled when she first had the memory.

On the first floor, he marched toward the security office, wishing he could personally go after Soto and bring him to justice. But his priority was to Kay—keeping her and Kaleb alive.

Drake knocked on the door to the room, and Pierce opened it. Drake peered at the security guard in front of a bank of security monitors. "I need to talk to you in private."

"We'll be right outside if you need me, John." Pierce moved into the corridor and closed the door. "How are Kaleb and Kay?"

"The doctor is hopeful Kaleb will make a full recovery. Kay's coping the best she can. In fact, the main reason I'm here is to tell you about what she has remembered. Her sister was murdered by her husband." Drake gave him the details Kay had told him.

Pierce scowled. "Does she know if he was involved in the *Muerte* Cartel?"

"No. She's been remembering bits and pieces of the nightmare. Today was the first time she saw the killer's face. Her sister wanted to get away from her husband, but she wouldn't tell Kay all the details or why—at least that she remembered. Just that he was abusive."

"I've been looking at a computer monitor too long." Pierce kneaded the side of his neck. "Soto has business ties in the US, and we've been delving into those ties. Most appear aboveboard, but there are two new ones that the FBI is investigating. What does your gut tell you?"

"At the least he's a murderer, but proving that might be hard, especially if Kay's sister can't be found."

"And not our job unless the crime occurred on US soil."

"No. Possibly in the home outside Juárez but he has several. It could be any of them."

"According to the Mexican authorities, he isn't at any of them. They even checked the one in Acapulco and the apartment in Mexico City." Pierce glanced up and down the hall. "He could be dead, too."

"Because of the *Muerte* Cartel or another one?"

"Yes, even if he wasn't part of one of them."

"Yeah, we need to consider all possibilities until we get evidence one way or another. Kay doesn't remember anything of her stay with her sister up until the murder. I think she'll recall more over the next few days."

"John is the head of hospital security. Let me introduce you."

Drake followed Pierce into the room. Pierce made the introductions, and Drake shook the security head's hand.

"I can change which camera I monitor. Right now, I have them on all the entrances and on the ones on the fifth floor. Everything is recorded and can be pulled up and reviewed if needed."

Drake shifted his focus from one monitor to the next, recognizing where some of the cameras were filming but not all. He pointed to a top left one. "Is this the only loading dock for the hospital?"

"Everything comes through there other than patients." John hit a key on his computer and changed the view. "There are two cameras capturing different angles."

"A police officer and a DEA agent are inspecting every item coming into the hospital," Pierce said as he gestured toward one man in uniform, then another a few yards away. The DEA agent was dressed as though he was a worker unloading the trucks.

Drake finished his perusal of the monitors and started to turn to leave. A tall, dark-haired man wearing a baseball cap, jeans and a University of Texas sweatshirt coming into the hospital through the main entrance caught his attention. There was something about how he carried himself—as if he owned the place—that gave Drake pause.

He pointed at the guy. "Have you seen that man before?"

John shook his head while Pierce said, "No."

"Can you zoom in on him?" Drake bent closer to the screen.

"This is the best I can do."

Drake stared at the man's right hand. Was that a gold ring—possibly like the one Soto had on in Kay's dream?

"I'm going to check him out." Drake couldn't explain exactly why. A gut feeling. "Keep an eye on him while I head for the lobby." He hurried from the security office and entered the lobby only a minute later.

But in that time, the tall man had disappeared. He called Pierce's cell phone. "Where did he go?"

"He got on elevator two and exited on the third floor. Do you want me to switch the monitors to follow him?"

"No. You're watching the essential places." If

it was Soto, it was more important to have the fifth floor locked down.

"I'll have John call the security guard on that floor and have him meet you at the elevator."

Drake rode the elevator up to the third floor, mentally preparing himself for an encounter. He kept thinking of the short video he'd been sent showing Soto from a distance leaving his office building in Juárez. People often changed their physical appearance but didn't think of things like how they walked or favorite mannerisms. By the time Drake got off the elevator, he was seventy percent sure Soto had just strolled into the hospital.

The young security guard approached Drake the second he exited the elevator. Although it looked like the suspicious man wore glasses under the baseball cap, Drake showed the guard a photo of Soto. "Have you seen him on this floor? He got off the elevator no more than a few minutes ago."

"No."

"Stay here. If you see a man wearing glasses, a baseball cap and a University of Texas sweat-shirt, call me here." Drake handed him a slip of paper with his cell phone number on it. "Do not approach or give away you're watching him. I'm searching the floor and want to know if he leaves."

The young man stood up straight. "Yes, sir. I can do that."

"Also keep an eye on the staircase at this end."

"Will do."

Drake went down each corridor and showed various employees Soto's photo while describing the guy he was looking for. One doctor thought he might have passed him, but he wasn't sure.

At the next nurses' station, an orderly pointed toward the second set of stairs at the opposite end from the bank of elevators. "Yeah, a minute ago. He was in a hurry."

"Thanks." Drake jogged toward the staircase door and eased it open, one hand near his holstered gun in case the man was waiting on the other side. He heard footsteps above him and below. If it was Soto, he would want to go up. Even with the guard on that door on the fifth floor, he decided to head that way. When he began up the steps, his cell phone rang. He quickly answered the call from Pierce.

"Drake, the silent alarm went off on the outside door in the first floor's west stairwell. Someone opened it and either went out or let a person inside."

"I'm a few floors above. I'll check it out." Drake turned and hurried down the steps.

"I have a police officer heading that way, too."

Drake stuffed his phone into his pocket and

quickened his pace. When he reached the bottom, an officer entered the stairwell. Drake shoved open the fire door that led outside and caught a glimpse of the man in question getting into a black sedan, which sped away. He ran forward, trying to get the tag number. The only numbers he saw were the last two—seven and four. Mud obscured the rest of the license plate.

The police officer came up behind him. "Was that the guy we're looking for?"

"Maybe." Drake strode toward the emergency exit. The fire door was shut and locked from the outside.

Had that been Soto? That man sure had walked like Kay's brother-in-law. If so, why had he come? To scout out the hospital? To taunt the police? Or something more sinister?

A diversion?

Urgency compelled him to move faster while placing a call to Dallas, stationed at Kaleb's hospital room.

With Drake gone, Kay couldn't even close her eyes, let alone sleep. Dallas stuck his head into the hospital room every once in a while, and she appreciated the gesture. She hadn't realized how much she'd come to depend on Drake's presence. She was remembering more pieces of her past life. As a firefighter, she'd faced many dangerous situations as part of her job, but in this case her life wasn't the only one on the line.

Kaleb slept in the baby bed inches from her. She sat next to it with the side railing down so she could soothe him when he became restless. She began to think she needed the physical connection more than he did.

What did a normal life feel like? Since Drake had left, she'd asked herself that question several times. She began to picture the firehouse she worked at and wondered if what she saw was right. Drake had shown her a photo of the outside of her house, but flashes of what the inside looked like started to form in her mind.

It was like the memory of her sister's murder had unplugged the dam holding her past back from her, and yet she couldn't remember what happened at her sister's house that led up to her death. Why did Kassandra's husband kill her? The memories she was having of her twin sister were filled with love and happiness.

She glanced at the clock on the wall. Where was Drake? He'd been gone over thirty minutes. She'd thought he would be back by now. If something had happened, surely Dallas would have informed her. She picked up the phone to call Drake, but halfway through punching in the number, she remembered he'd said he would be gone an hour and hung up.

Her eyelids felt heavy. She laid her head on Kaleb's bed near him and placed her hand on his arm. Maybe she would close her eyes for a few minutes.

But she wouldn't go to sleep. She couldn't relive Kassandra's death again.

A hand clasping her shoulder jerked her awake. She popped up, glancing over her shoulder—at Drake. She jumped up and threw her arms around him. "You're all right."

"Yes. I know I was gone over an hour, but—"

"An hour?" Kay checked the clock on the wall. "I must have fallen asleep. I wasn't going to. I…"

"Was tired?"

She nodded.

Drake embraced her. "I was making sure the security was in place. Nothing is going to happen to you two."

The fervent last statement made her wonder if something had happened while he was gone. "Anything suspicious?"

"One guy who came into the hospital had the same build as Soto. I went to check him out."

"Who was he?"

"He left before I could talk to him. I did get a partial tag number and make of the vehicle he was in. Pierce is running what little we know through the system to see if anything comes up."

"That sounds like a long shot."

"It is. The man is gone, and the guards have been alerted." Drake turned toward the bed. "How's Kaleb?"

"Moving more. The nurse told me the doctor would be here soon to examine him."

"Good. I hope he can give us an estimate of when Kaleb can leave the hospital. I'll feel better when he can."

She felt the same way. What little she could recall about Kassandra's husband didn't bode well. She'd started to remember part of her sister's wedding. Alejandro Soto had been charming, but there were a couple of times when he'd wanted something a certain way and Kassandra hadn't. Looking back, Kay realized he'd always gotten his way.

A memory flitted through her mind. When she'd arrived at Kassandra's house over Thanksgiving, her sister had hugged her tightly and started to tell her something, but she'd stopped when her husband joined them in the foyer. When she'd looked between Alejandro and Kassandra, Kay's two overriding impressions had been that her sister was scared and her husband had had no idea that Kassandra had asked her to come visit. And a few days later, those assumptions had been proven true.

* * *

The bright light of a new day streamed through the narrow slits in the blinds, enticing Kay to open them. She even took a step toward the window. But Drake's words from yesterday about a possible sniper stopped her. She missed being outside in the sunlight. Her freedom of movement was stifled as much as a prisoner in a cell.

In two days, she hadn't left Kaleb's hospital room. Stroking his back, Kay held him close to her as she walked from one end of the small confines to the other. The pediatrician would be in soon to let her know when he thought it would be safe for Kaleb to leave the hospital.

"It won't be long before we can go, Kaleb." She gently returned him to the baby bed and took her post right next to him in a chair with the railing lowered.

He held her finger, brought it to his mouth and proceeded to gum it. She felt the edge of the tooth coming in.

"After the doctor comes, you'll get to eat. Just hold on for a little while."

Kaleb gibbered.

Thank goodness he didn't know she wasn't Kassandra. He didn't need to deal with the loss of his mother with all that was going on. When he was older, she would tell him. She wouldn't let his father come near Kaleb, if at all possible.

When the door swung open, Drake entered with Dr. Santos.

Kay rose and stepped away to let the doctor examine Kaleb. He tolerated Dr. Santos's probing, only trying to wiggle away at the end. She put her hand on the top of Kaleb's head to calm him. He immediately found her watch and tugged on the band.

The pediatrician backed away and picked up the chart to scribble notes down. "Unless there's a problem, he can go home this afternoon after a few more tests. I'm taking him off his IV."

"That's great." Kay slanted a look at Drake. The relief on his face matched how she felt.

After Dr. Santos left, a nurse came into the room and removed the IV. "I'm glad to see he's doing so much better."

Kay smiled. "He had us worried, but he's a little tiger. He doesn't stay down for long."

"The doctor said you'd be leaving a little later."

"Yes. I appreciate all your help with Kaleb."

As the young nurse walked to the door, Kay returned to her chair and scooped up Kaleb to hold. "Since he's been up most of the morning, I'm going to try to get him to take a nap so he'll be rested when we leave." As she held him against her chest, she rocked back and forth. "Did the police find anything about the guy you thought might be my sister's husband in the stolen car they found this morning?"

"Wiped clean. It was abandoned in an area where there weren't any cameras and no one was willing to come forward. When So—the man and his accomplice drove away, only one traffic cam caught the vehicle and that was near the hospital. Nothing from that picture can help us. They were careful, which only reinforces my feeling that was Soto in the passenger seat." Near Kay, Drake leaned back against the baby bed, partially perched on it.

"All the more reason to leave here today."

"I'll need to check with Pierce later this afternoon before we leave the hospital. I think the diversion we've planned could help us catch him. Once we're away and not being followed, we should be okay. Again, Dallas will accompany us, and our location will only be known to us and Pierce."

"A new safe house?"

"Yes, in El Paso area in case Kaleb has a problem. We'll be close to medical care."

Kay glanced at Kaleb, who had fallen asleep. "I think I'll try to take a nap while he is. Later it might be hectic." She stood and carefully placed the baby in the bed while Drake helped her lift the railing.

As she straightened, Drake clasped her arm and tugged her closer. "A lot of people here and in Mexico are looking for Soto."

He looked away for a few seconds, and when his gaze returned to her face, she realized he had something else to tell her from his conversation with Pierce earlier. And suddenly she knew what it was. "Kassandra's body was found."

He nodded. "The Mexican authorities discovered another piece of property, a ranch he owned. The ranch house had burned down a couple of days before. They found a woman's body in what would have been the master bedroom. No confirmation it was your sister yet. The fire wasn't reported, and because its location was isolated, no one else came forward about what happened. There were also a male and female body in the stable, which caught fire, too. The male doesn't fit Soto's build or height, and they could tell from the woman she most likely wasn't your sister."

"A fire? I don't remember anything like that."

"You could have been gone by then."

"Or I don't recall that part of what went down."

"The bottom line is we think Soto has gone underground, and very likely in the United

States. He never officially crossed the border, but there are other ways. He has the connections and money to make that happen, especially if he's coming for his son."

Kay shivered at the thought of a murderer taking Kaleb. She didn't care that the man was Kaleb's father. If she had to disappear to give Kaleb a chance to grow up a normal little boy, she would.

Drake tightened his arms around Kay. "I'm not going to let that happen, Kay. I care about Kaleb too much to have him ever returned to his father." He kissed the top of her head, his hand stroking her back. When he pulled away slightly, he stared at her.

His look melted her, her legs giving way. He supported her at the same time as he dipped his head toward hers.

A loud boom shook the room—the whole building—a picture on the wall crashed to the floor. Multiple alarms rang.

FOURTEEN

Stunned, Drake held Kay against him for a few heartbeats, trying to process what had just happened. A bomb?

The lights flickered and went off.

Kaleb's cries pierced through Drake's daze, and he set a shocked Kay in a nearby chair and then went to the bed and picked up the baby. He cradled him like a football against his chest and opened the blinds to let some daylight into the room.

As the door swung open, he quickly passed Kaleb to Kay and put his hand on his gun. Dallas rushed inside. Behind him, people hurried up and down the hall.

"The transformer blew up. The backup generator should come on any second."

"Blew up?" Could this be the work of Soto? "We have to get out of here."

Some lights came back on.

Drake breathed a little easier, because the

stairs were the only way to leave the floor. Now they would be able to see the steps they would descend and also if anyone was waiting for them.

"Kay, get everything you need for Kaleb. We're leaving."

"You think this is Soto's doing?"

"I don't know for sure, but I'm not taking any chances. We're going to implement our plan a bit earlier."

Kay stuffed everything she'd brought of Kaleb's as well as items they had acquired while in the hospital. Drake helped her secure Kaleb against her using the baby sling while Dallas opened the door and checked the corridor.

"The staff is going into emergency mode. Not as chaotic as before."

"Let's go. We'll use the south stairwell." Drake informed Pierce of their plans, then removed his gun from its holster.

Dallas stepped out first and motioned them forward, then they headed for the exit. When Drake opened the door to the stairs, he scanned the lit area, then entered and flattened himself against the wall while looking up. Dallas positioned himself at the railing and looked down. The sound of footsteps echoed through the stairwell. A young man and woman appeared from the sixth floor and hastened past them. More joined them.

Drake pushed his way into the flow between a family with a child about eight or nine and an older couple. Drake descended first with Kay following right behind him and Dallas taking up the rear. A crowd could help them, but that also made it harder to keep tabs on everyone.

Drake hurried, but he couldn't set the pace as fast as the group's because Kaleb didn't need to be jarred with his stitches. Some people passed them on the steps. He'd feel better when they were away from the hospital.

At the third-floor landing, another explosion reverberated through the building, and what lighting they had went out. Total darkness entombed them. Someone screamed from above.

"Hold on to the railing," Drake whispered to Kay, then withdrew his cell phone and tapped his flashlight app on, while others did the same around him.

With the second explosion most likely affecting the generator, even more people flooded the stairwell. In their rush to get out of the hospital, pandemonium began to drive some of the people behind him. A tall, rugged-looking man, his head poking above the rest, shoved his way toward them. Drake twisted toward Kay, keeping his gaze fastened on the guy, and stopped their progress until the stranger passed them. As he did, he looked Kay up and down. Drake moved his hand stuck in his jacket enough for the man to glimpse his Texas Ranger star and gun. With a glare, he pressed forward, leaving them behind.

But that didn't mean the guy wouldn't be waiting for them at the bottom.

Kay leaned close. "What's wrong?"

When the mob knocked an older woman into Kay, jostling Kaleb, he whimpered. Kay helped support the lady until she got her footing. Kaleb began crying.

"I'm so sorry. Is he all right?" the stranger asked.

"Yes, just surprised." Kay used her body to shield the fragile woman until a large man plunged through the multitude.

"Grandma, you okay?"

"Thanks to her." The lady nodded toward Kay, then latched onto her grandson, who took Kay's position of guarding his grandmother.

Drake glanced at Kay, who immediately returned her focus on Kaleb. "We're almost to the bottom. If you have to, hold on to the back of my jacket."

On the first floor, even more people crammed the small space, all trying to get through the single exit to the outside. Screams and shouts filled the stairwell. Drake veered in the direction of the door into the hospital. He felt the tug on his jacket as Kay battled to stay right behind him.

The hard part was wedging himself through the entrance while others wanted out. He received glares and frowns, but he kept going, trying not to get caught up in the raging river of people determined to escape. He grasped Kay's hand and sidestepped through the throng. When he burst free of the human plug at the door, he pulled Kay to him, then kept going in the direction of the security office, where Pierce was waiting to help with the plan that they had come up with earlier to get Kay and Kaleb out of the hospital—Drake hoped undetected.

Pierce stood by the door, a flashlight in his hand. "No use staring at blank TV screens." He started toward the back of the building. A few stragglers passed them in the hall. Dallas kept his attention on them while Drake concentrated on who was in front of them.

"The hearse is parked at the loading bay. Some patients are being moved to safety from there, so it will be hectic." Pierce stopped at the entrance to the morgue while Drake took Kay and Kaleb into the room.

Kay stared at the gurney with a black body bag on it. "Did I tell you I think I'm claustrophobic?"

"No, but if someone is watching the exits, they won't be sure you and Kaleb are in the bag. It'll give you two a better chance to get away without anyone trailing us. It's your choice."

She turned her back on Drake so he could assist her with getting out of the baby sling. Then while Drake held Kaleb, she climbed onto the stainless-steel table. Kaleb didn't take his gaze off Kay. As she lay down, his mouth screwed up in a frown. He let out a cry.

Kay opened her arms, and Drake nestled Kaleb against her side. "I'll leave the very top unzipped. When you're in the hearse and away from the hospital, the driver will tell you and you can open it farther."

"Okay." She rose and leaned over to kiss Kaleb on the forehead. "We're gonna be all right, sweetie."

Drake wanted to kiss Kay, but he had to shove that thought away. There was no place for emotions right now. He would see her soon—he prayed.

As he zipped up the body bag, the last thing he saw was Kay's large dark brown eyes. A police officer dressed as an orderly wheeled the gurney out of the morgue. Pierce followed them at a distance while Drake and Dallas went back to the security room and knocked on the door. A female Texas Ranger, dressed like Kay with a light brown wig on, opened the door.

"Ready?" Drake asked.

She nodded, grabbed a large blanket-wrapped doll and held it against her. "Yes."

Dallas chuckled. "Abbey, I never thought you would be holding a baby."

She shot him a withering look, then took dark sunglasses and a baseball cap from Dallas. "It's just a prop, like these are. That's the closest I'll ever get to the real thing."

Drake shook his head and strode toward an exit near the front by the visitors' parking lot. Abbey kept the fake baby up close to her face. If Soto was after his son, he wouldn't risk shooting her while she held "Kaleb" like that.

When Drake reached the SUV he would be using, he huddled close to Abbey as she slipped into the back seat of the car with dark tinted windows. The stench of smoke drifted on the light breeze. As he rounded the front, he panned the area for any sign of Soto or his thugs.

Dallas came around the other side and climbed in behind Drake in the driver's seat. He started the car, headed to the street and pulled out into traffic. The vicinity around the hospital was blocked off while firefighters and police swarmed the building.

As Drake drove away from the chaotic scene, he centered his attention on the traffic in front and to the left of the SUV while Dallas did behind and to the right.

Three blocks away, Dallas said, "There's a white van behind us. It's been there since the hospital."

Drake made a sudden sharp left at a yellow light, then a hundred yards away took another left, then a right.

"It's gone." Dallas paused. "No, wait it's still back there, and another car is behind the van. They may be together."

"It's time we make our stand." Drake followed a series of turns, pushing the speed limit as much as he could. "We're almost at our destination."

"Both the car and van are still on our tail."

Drake spied the row of warehouses ahead. The abandoned one at the end was where they would make their stand against Soto and his cohorts. Several DEA agents were waiting inside.

From the other end of the warehouses, a black pickup drove toward Drake. A third vehicle? He couldn't take the chance. He spied an opening up ahead and raced to make it.

He made a hard right and ran into a dead end. He slammed on the brakes, and the SUV fishtailed, the building only feet from them. Drake turned the wheel so the side of the car would be facing their pursuers, missing the barrier by a few inches.

The van came around the corner first and

stopped while the vehicle behind it blocked off their escape.

"Get out!" Drake scrambled from the SUV, grabbing his rifle as backup.

Abbey, minus her disguise and baby, did the same with Dallas right behind her.

Trapped, Drake positioned himself behind the front tire, using the hood as cover.

As the police officer wheeled Kay and Kaleb to the loading dock, she felt sealed tightly in the body bag. When the gurney went through the double doors and down what must be a ramp, only one small opening let dim light into the bag. She could barely make out Kaleb in the crook of her arm, quiet for the moment. Added to the trapped feeling, alarms and sirens bombarded her. The dark cocoon seemed to calm the baby, even as her heart beat at a maddeningly fast rate. Her chest rose and fell rapidly as she dragged in sips of stale air.

Who had lain in this bag before her?

The question sent her mind toward a full-fledged panic.

She couldn't let that happen. She quickly centered her thoughts on Drake. He and Dallas had set up a decoy to entice anyone looking for her to follow. If the plan worked, Soto and his men could be captured shortly.

She needed the nightmare to end.

Suddenly the gurney was lifted and shoved into what must be the hearse on its way to a funeral home. The jostling roused Kaleb.

He moved, babbling.

"Shh, Kaleb."

"Mama," he said, clearer than ever before.

The word brought tears to her eyes. Kassandra was gone.

The back door to the hearse slammed shut. Kay rolled partially onto her side and cuddled Kaleb against her. "I'm here, Kaleb." She lowered her head within the confining bag and kissed the top of his head. "I love you. We're going to be all right."

The sound of another door closing and the engine starting was her signal she could lower the zipper a little more to let fresh air inside. She did, then stroked Kaleb. "See, we're out of the hospital and safe."

His hand reached up and explored the contours of her face, as if Kaleb were reassuring himself that his mama was with him. She'd loved being a twin, but in this moment, she was even more grateful. The sight of her would give Kaleb stability in a world gone mad—much like Drake had been a comfort to her when she didn't even know who she was.

As the hearse drove away from the hospital,

there was a lot of stop and go until they were blocks away from the commotion. The funeral home was on the other side of El Paso, according to Drake a thirty-minute ride. It didn't take Kaleb long to fall asleep again. Soon, with the smooth ride, fresh air and light around her, Kay couldn't fight the heaviness of her own eyelids. They slid closed, and she relaxed for the first time today.

The sound of a door closing dragged her awake, followed by two male voices, talking quietly. Kay lifted her head to peek out the dark window at where they were. A white brick building dominated the scenery. Not far away another hearse was parked.

Then her gaze latched on the two men talking—one was the driver and the other Texas Ranger Pierce. Their frowns and furrowed brows warned her something had gone wrong with the plan.

After placing a call to Pierce, Drake rose and pulled the trigger, then ducked back down. A shot struck the wall behind him. There were at least six assailants. The DEA agents were only two warehouses away. Even with the sounds from the gunfire, he had Pierce call and let them know they were trapped in a dead-end alley. With the SUV the only barrier between them and Soto's men, he didn't know how long they could last. Their vehicle was riddled with bullets, and behind them was a brick wall with one door, bolted, in it. Even if they could get inside, in order to make it to the entrance, they would have to run two or three yards in the open.

When two guys climbed into the truck and backed away, Drake fired repeatedly at the truck's windshield, which shattered. But he missed both of the assailants, and they left the scene. A barrage of bullets from the remaining four kept them pinned down.

Why did they leave? To get more help?

Drake glanced over his shoulder and saw a window on the second floor above the door. Were the two men moving around front and breaking into the warehouse so they could come up behind them? A plan began to form in his mind. He wouldn't let them be ambushed that way. Besides, if he could get into the warehouse, he could use the window for a better shooting advantage.

"Abbey. Dallas." Drake spoke low, hoping to get his partners' attention without letting their attackers know.

Abbey turned toward him. "I'm running out of ammo."

When Dallas looked their way, Drake quickly told them his plan to make it to the door, open it and get inside before being shot. "I need you both to shoot at the four remaining guys at the same time."

"Three now. I just shot one." Dallas changed the clip in his gun.

"Good. Better odds." Drake told them about his suspicions concerning the two men who'd left. "After I shoot the lock, I'm going to make a break for the door. Just keep them pinned down for thirty seconds."

Drake swiveled around and aimed for the door's lock. It burst apart and fell to the asphalt. While Dallas and Abbey fired, Drake dashed toward the back of the building. When he reached the entrance and jerked it open, a bullet struck a brick inches from him. He dived inside.

Drake quickly moved through the small warehouse's first floor, then hurried up the stairs and found the window that overlooked the dead-end alley. He cranked it open, steadied his rifle on the sill and targeted one of the assailants near the front of the van. The bullet hit his right shoulder, and the guy went down. He quickly searched for another vulnerable attacker and sighted him in his scope, but before he could fire his weapon, three cars converged on the scene.

Kay wiggled free of the body bag and knocked on the hearse window to get Pierce's attention.

He turned toward her, said something to the police officer, then came to the vehicle and opened the back door.

"What happened?" Kay asked before he could say anything.

"Got a call from Drake. They're pinned down in a dead-end alley with six attackers shooting at them."

Too many people had already died. "Then we've got to help them."

"Backup is on the way to them. The one thing he wanted me to do is get you to the safe house and protect you."

"You think they followed both vehicles?" She picked up Kaleb and held him close.

"No, but we have to act as though that's possible. The police officer will stay here and let me know if anyone comes. But right now, our concern is your safety." Pierce offered her his hand and helped her from the hearse. She reached in and grabbed her backpack with their belongings that had been in the body bag.

She climbed into the back of the Texas Ranger's vehicle with Kaleb. Pierce drove away from the funeral home while Kay crouched behind the driver's seat with her nephew in her arms.

"Who knows where the safe house is?"

"Only four Texas Rangers—me, Dallas, Drake

and Flynn Winchester. He's there now to make sure the place hasn't been compromised."

"Compromised? You think Alejandro knows about it?"

"Since we didn't even decide on the exact location until an hour ago, not likely. Flynn has been posted there since we implemented the escape. No one in any other law enforcement agency knows. The fewer the better."

Lord, please protect Drake and the others. I wish I could do more, but it's in Your hands now.

The DEA agents swarmed the alley, turning the tables on the assailants. Dallas and Abbey moved in from one side while Drake covered them from the second-floor window. He took down another thug before the last two surrendered. When the scene was secured, he rushed downstairs, keeping alert in case the two that had driven away returned.

Outside, Abbey worked with the DEA agents to take the assailants in while Drake and Dallas climbed into the bullet-riddled SUV.

"I hope this car makes it to the garage," Drake muttered as he steered the vehicle through the narrow opening at the end of the alley.

Once clear of the area, Drake called Pierce and told him what happened. "There are two assailants in a black truck that left. I couldn't tell if Soto was one of them. Have someone check the traffic cams in this area for around eleven thirty to see if they can pick it up. After getting a new vehicle, we'll be coming to the safe house."

"We're almost there, and I haven't seen anyone tailing us. See you soon." Pierce disconnected.

"Soto is still out there. I feel like we're back to square one." Drake slanted a look at Dallas.

His partner frowned. "Something doesn't feel right."

"I agree. We were supposed to be leading them into a trap. But instead, we ended up trapped in that dead-end alley."

"It's like they knew what we had planned. We only devised that plan this morning, since there was a good chance Kaleb would be released today." Their conversation had been between Dallas, him and Kay. Then he'd called Pierce on his cell phone and told him to make the arrangement. The DEA agents hadn't been dispatched earlier than planned until the transformer went. "They had to have time to put their end together. We need to have Kaleb's hospital room checked for a bug."

"The only people allowed into the room were a couple of nurses and the doctor."

"I hope I'm wrong, but we need to know one way or another."

Dallas withdrew his cell phone. "I'll call Abbey and have her get to the hospital right away and check the room for bugs."

"The one thing we didn't talk about in the room was where the safe house was located."

Dallas placed a call to Abbey and arranged for her to inspect the room.

"If she doesn't find anything, that doesn't mean someone didn't bug the place. In the middle of the evacuation and all the confusion, the person could have come back into the room and removed it. Soto got the information he needed to set a trap."

"I wish we knew more about Soto. Has Kay remembered anything besides that he killed her sister?"

Drake shook his head. "Not about Soto. Just memories from her past."

"Something made her hide in her sister's bedroom when Soto came inside."

"Yes, I think she's blocking another memory. When she talks about him, her voice is full of fear."

After leaving the SUV and picking up a four-wheel-drive Jeep, Drake headed for the safe house. The last time he'd talked with Pierce five minutes ago, everything was fine. They had arrived with no incident and the place was secured.

He needed to see Kay, hold her and reassure

her he would be there for her. The more he discovered about Soto, the more troubled he was. Men like Soto who didn't value a human being's life were the same as the ones he'd encountered in the human trafficking market. All they wanted was money and power. People didn't matter.

Halfway to the new safe house, Drake's cell phone rang, and he answered the call from Abbey. "Was there a listening device in Kaleb's hospital room?"

"No, but I got a list of the people who went into the room while Kaleb was there. I'm tracking down the ones who were here today. I'm going to do some digging into those first. I'll let you know what I find out."

"Thanks. We're almost to the safe house." Drake ended the call and told Dallas what Abbey said.

"If there wasn't a bug, then how did they know to set up an ambush at the warehouse?"

"Good question. There still could be the possibility that a bug was in the room until the evacuation." Drake turned into a driveway and parked in front of the garage next to Pierce's SUV, then grabbed his duffel bag. The beauty of this place was a glassed-in turret that gave a 360-degree view of the area, coupled with a top-notch security system.

Pierce opened the door before Drake could ring the bell. "Kay finally got Kaleb down for a nap."

When he moved into the house, Kay appeared in the entrance from the living room. Relief mixed with fatigue on her face. He smiled. She did, too, and her expression transformed her features for a few seconds before the gravity of her situation intruded again.

As Pierce left, Dallas came into the house. "This is definitely a step up."

"There was something about the cabin I really liked," Kay said, her gaze still trained on Drake.

"It was cramped?" Dallas closed and locked the front door.

Kay chuckled. "No, it was cozy."

"I figure you two have some catching up to do. I'm claiming my bedroom, then checking in with Flynn before I get the lay of the land."

Drake dropped his duffel bag in the entry hall and approached Kay. "It's been crazy. Are you all right?"

"Better now that we're here. I know when I'm tense Kaleb senses it, and he becomes fussy. Thankfully he didn't really make any noise until Pierce was driving us here. He never said a word, but Kaleb screamed for about ten minutes straight the last part of the trip. Poor guy. I don't think he's been around kids."

"He's not married. I get the impression from working with him he's a confirmed bachelor."

"Then that ride probably only confirmed that in his mind." Kay took a seat on the couch, collapsing back on the cushion with a long sigh. "I'm exhausted, but I don't think I can sleep a wink."

"Me, too. It's been a busy day, and it's only midafternoon." Drake sat next to her.

"I need to call the doctor and make sure I understand all the instructions for Kaleb."

"I'll have Pierce do it. I don't want anyone tracing our calls to this place."

"Pierce told me a little about what happened earlier. Was Soto at the ambush?"

"Maybe. A truck with two men was there for a short time. I only got a good look at the driver. They left right after the shootout began."

Kay lowered her head and rubbed her thumb in her hand. "Alejandro is evil. I remembered something else I witnessed in Mexico. I love horses and decided to go see my brother-in-law's stable—he had some very expensive Thoroughbreds. I'd been cooped up in the main house since I arrived and needed fresh air, although Kassandra insisted I stay inside. I knew something was terribly wrong, but I couldn't get her to tell me anything. In fact, she only wanted me to stay a couple of days. Originally I was going to visit for a week."

"She didn't tell you why?"

"No, but then, Alejandro rarely left us alone. If he did, someone else was nearby. I got up early while everyone was asleep and went to the stable. I was in a stall with Kassandra's horse when men came in, dragging an older woman and man. They murdered both of them. I think one of the guys saw me running back to the house. I'm the reason Alejandro killed Kassandra. If only I'd stayed in the house..." Her voice trailed off into silence.

Drake cupped the side of her face with one hand. "You aren't to blame. Alejandro is. Don't let him have that kind of power over you." With a thumb, he brushed a tear from her cheek. "How did you end up witnessing her death?"

"I was in her room, trying to get her to run away with me. She'd packed a backpack with Kaleb's things, and we were going to sneak away in the middle of the night. She made me promise to go with Kaleb, no matter what. She wanted the world to know what kind of man Alejandro really was." Kay swallowed hard. "I was in the baby's nursery when Alejandro burst into her room and..." More tears fell from her eyes. "You know the rest. I didn't catch everything he shouted at Kassandra. I know Spanish, but he was talking rapidly. Plus, I was scared and shaking."

He clasped her shoulders. "It's useless to blame yourself." But wasn't that what he was doing with Beth's disappearance? For years, he'd centered his life on finding answers to what had happened to her, when he most likely would never discover the truth. Then Shanna had been murdered. After that, he'd stopped living—just gone through the motions each day.

He slowly leaned forward, kissing each of her tearstained cheeks. "You're giving Kaleb a chance to live like a normal child."

"Not as long as Alejandro is free to terrorize people."

"That's why we're going to catch him and put him away."

"With what evidence? Mine? That happened in Mexico."

"It'll work out." Somehow. He couldn't stand seeing Kay hurt so much.

He pulled her close, and she laid her cheek against his chest—until his cell phone rang. He retrieved it from his pocket and looked at who was calling. "I've got to take this."

She moved away and rose. "I'm going to check on Kaleb."

He answered Abbey's call when Kay disappeared into the hallway. "Did you find out anything?"

"Yes, the nurse who was on shift on Kaleb's floor and took care of him was found dead in the parking garage at the hospital. Her throat was slashed."

"You think she's connected to Soto and that's why she was murdered?"

"Yes. Too much of a coincidence."

"Agreed, which makes me wonder who else Soto recruited to get information about where Kay and Kaleb are."

FIFTEEN

Kay slowed her pace and caught Drake's words to someone on the phone. *Who else has died because Soto is after me?*

Since she woke up at the hospital over a week ago, her life had been a living nightmare, and Kaleb was in the middle of it all. Even worse were her returning memories. She needed to remember and yet wished she hadn't. Reliving her twin's murder was like witnessing her own death over and over.

And she'd started it all when she went to the stable and saw the couple being killed. Too many deaths. All she wanted to do was take Kaleb and disappear. She didn't want anyone else to be hurt because of her. Not realizing what she was doing, she'd poked a rattlesnake, and he'd struck back.

Kay escaped to the bedroom and sat in a chair, watching Kaleb sleeping in the baby bed next to her. Kaleb thought she was Kassandra, his mama. "Sweetie, I promise I'll do everything I can to be a good mother for you. That's the least I can do. When we can, we'll leave and go somewhere no one can find us."

The thought of not seeing Drake anymore saddened her, but she wouldn't put him in danger, too. He was close to his family, and he loved his job.

But she couldn't shake the feelings he stirred in her.

I love him.

The realization stunned her. She'd dated in the past and been serious with two men, but they had never made her feel like Drake did—cherished, protected, a person she could share her soul and heart with. Even if he felt the same way, she couldn't ask him to spend a life on the run. Alejandro would never stop hunting her, even if he was caught. He'd find a way to reach her.

With her mind settled on what she would do, she rose, kissed her fingertips and touched Kaleb on the top of his head.

When Flynn relieved Drake on guard duty, he came downstairs from the top floor, where he'd been watching the terrain around the house, which sat on an acre of land with few places for people to hide within a hundred yards. Beyond that distance were clusters of trees and bushes.

He'd preferred the whole area being clear, but the security system was good and there were three of them to protect Kay and Kaleb, which allowed one to be downstairs and the other in the turret. The third would be off duty but there if needed.

This was his time to relax as much as he could and later possibly catch some sleep. But first he wanted to see Kay about Abbey's call. Kay wanted to know what was going on, and she deserved that, but he hadn't had a chance since earlier this afternoon to tell her about the nurse. When Kay left to check on Kaleb, she hadn't returned to the living room. He wasn't surprised she had decided to nap, but he missed seeing her.

Kay has become very important to me. And so has Kaleb.

When Drake entered the living room, he found her sitting on the edge of a blanket spread on the floor, her back to him. He paused in the entrance. Kaleb played with a couple of toys she'd bought for him, putting them in his mouth and gumming them. When her nephew finally flung the teething ring away, Kay picked up Mr. Teddy and held him up, shaking him in front of Kaleb. For several seconds, the baby followed the dancing stuffed animal, then reached up and grabbed its arm.

"Oh, so you want to play tug-of-war with me," she said in a teasing voice.

Kaleb giggled.

"You've got your work cut out for you." Kay pulled on Mr. Teddy.

With a smile taking over his whole face, Kaleb held on to the stuffed animal, coming slightly off the floor. Kay put a hand under him in case he suddenly let go. He didn't.

"You're getting to be so strong, but I'm gonna win." Kay laughed, the sound wonderful to hear.

"No, you aren't. Us guys have to stick together." Drake covered the distance to the blanket and knelt next to Kaleb. The baby looked at him, his eyes twinkling with mischief.

"Two against one. That's not fair." She gave him a pretend frown.

"You can use both hands, and I'll make sure Kaleb doesn't fall back."

"You two are on." Kay clasped one arm and Mr. Teddy's head.

A tug-of-war ensued, Drake making sure he only used enough strength to keep Kaleb in the game. The baby giggled again.

When the stuffed animal tore partway at the armpit, Kay's eyes grew big, and she immediately released her hold. Drake supported Kaleb as he lowered him to the blanket, clutching Mr. Teddy with a dangling arm.

"I broke it. Can I see it?" Kay asked Kaleb, and when she took Mr. Teddy, he let go. "I should be able to sew it…" Her voice trailed off as she withdrew a flash drive. She glanced at Drake. "What's a flash…" Her eyes narrowed on the object in her hand. "Kassandra put it there. I'm sure of it."

"Let's see. I have my laptop. I've hooked it into the security system to monitor the cameras. It's up in the turret."

Kay passed the flash drive to Drake. "I haven't been up. Now's a good time to see the view, right before the sun sets."

"Did you meet Flynn yet?" He stood.

"No." She took his offered hand, and he pulled her to her feet.

Then he scooped up Kaleb, who patted his beard stubble and became fascinated by the rough texture along Drake's jawline. "We're going on an adventure."

Kay followed Drake and Kaleb up two flights of stairs. When she entered the turret, her gaze fixed on the splashes of orange, pink and rose on the western horizon. "Beautiful."

"Yeah, it definitely tempts a person to stare at it rather than work, but don't worry, I'm resisting its lure." A blond-haired man about Drake's height held his hand out to her. "I'm Flynn Winchester."

She shook it. "Thanks for being here."

"What brings y'all up here?" Flynn went back

to his post, using binoculars to search for anything suspicious.

"We discovered a flash drive in Kaleb's stuffed animal. I want to see if I can open it." Drake passed the baby boy to Kay, then crossed to the open laptop on a counter, displaying four pictures of various areas outside the house.

He stuck the flash drive into the USB port and opened it. "It's encrypted, but I'll send it to Pierce and see if he can find someone to hack into it." He retrieved his cell phone and called headquarters. He told Pierce about what they found.

"Send it. We'll see what we can discover. The information on it could be important."

"Yeah, that's what I thought, especially since Soto is going to such lengths to locate Kay and Kaleb. It could be more than just wanting his son back. He doesn't seem like the warm fuzzy type."

Pierce laughed, but nothing was funny about the sound. "Far from it. Not with the bodies left behind where he's gone. I'll let you know what we discover."

Drake attached the flash drive folder to an email and sent it. "Did you get the file?"

"Yes. The four guys we caught at the ambush are being guarded. We want to keep them alive. If one of them talks, I'll let you know. Which reminds me, Captain Vincent called an hour ago. He thinks the only way the assailant who died from poisoning could have obtained the cyanide was through his lawyer. That man, who was supposed to be from San Antonio, has disappeared. Captain Vincent discovered there isn't an attorney in Texas by his name."

"Thanks. He's probably right." Drake twisted away from Kay and lowered his voice. "He goes out of his way to leave no loose ends."

When he disconnected, he faced Kay, realizing he still had to tell her about the nurse and the lawyer. "Let's go downstairs. I don't want to keep Flynn distracted from his job."

As they left, Kay said, "Thanks, Flynn. I appreciate your help."

When they returned to the living room, Kay put Kaleb on the blanket and sat next to him while the boy held Mr. Teddy minus the one arm. "He doesn't seem to mind its missing part."

Drake eased down on the other side of Kaleb. "What do you think is on the flash drive?"

"When Alejandro returned to the ranch and confronted my sister that afternoon, he kept shouting, 'What did you do with it?' He might not have known about me at the stable. He could have been talking about the flash drive. Maybe that's what put him into a rage."

"I'm hoping it has intel about the *Muerte* Cartel on it, especially concerning its ties to the United States." He cleared his throat and told her about the lawyer and the cyanide.

She shivered. "Anyone who threatens Soto doesn't live."

"Also one of the nurses who looked after Kaleb was found dead at the hospital."

"Murdered?"

"Yes. We believe she placed a listening device in Kaleb's room. That would explain why we were ambushed at the warehouses."

"Did you find one in the room?"

"No, but since she was on duty today and in Kaleb's room, she could have removed it when we evacuated. It wasn't on her, but whoever killed her could have taken the device. She received a large amount of money in her bank account two days ago. Pierce is tracking the money trail."

"My brother-in-law has a long reach. I hope the flash drive has the information to take him down. No one else should die because of that man."

"I wish I had good information for you."

Kay leaned across Kaleb and took Drake's hand. "I'm going to have to disappear. I won't let Kaleb grow up in that man's care."

"Right now there's a manhunt for him. Let's

hope he can be found." He hoped so, because living on the run, always looking over your shoulder, was no way to live.

As Kay left her bedroom later after putting Kaleb down for the night, the stress of the day had a stranglehold on her. She planned to rest as long as Kaleb allowed her to, but first she wanted to find out what Pierce had discovered on the flash drive—if anything.

She entered the kitchen, where Drake was making another pot of coffee. His shift downstairs would begin soon. After their conversation concerning the nurse, she had insisted Drake get some sleep. She'd wanted to spend as much time with him as possible but realized that would only make their parting harder.

He looked up from pouring coffee into a mug and smiled.

"Did Pierce have any news?"

"I didn't talk to him. He was in the captain's office, but he'll call me back when he returns to his desk. I have a good feeling about this. He wouldn't be talking with the captain unless he discovered something—" His ringing cell phone interrupted him. Stepping away, he quickly answered it, saying, "Jackson here," as he set his mug on the table. The earlier smile grew as he listened to whoever called. "Let me know how the raid goes. Maybe Soto will get caught up—"

Suddenly the lights went out, reminding Kay of the hospital earlier. "Drake?" She felt for the counter nearby to help get her bearings.

"My phone and my com earpiece to Dallas and Flynn are dead, too. Dallas," Drake shouted.

He answered, the sound coming from the living room. "Stay where you are. I'll be there. I can't get Flynn on my com," he finished, sounding closer—he must have stepped into the kitchen. "Where are you?"

"I'm here," Kay said while Drake answered, too, but farther away from her than a moment earlier.

"I've got our night-vision goggles. I'll bring you yours, Dallas. Then check out front and the left side while I take the back and right. I'll check the alarm."

Drake's voice came closer as he talked with Dallas. He touched her arm. "Come with me." He took her hand and moved forward, guiding her through the kitchen door into the hallway. "We'll start with your bedroom on the right so you can get Kaleb. You two need to stay in the bathroom in the center of the house. No outside walls."

While he led her down the corridor, her heartbeat thudded so loudly she wondered if he could hear it.

"I wish I had another set of night-vision goggles."

Flynn came down the stairs. "We're under attack. I count eight coming in from the right, back and front. I tried to call headquarters. I can't."

"I'm taking Kay and Kaleb to the interior bathroom across from Dallas's room upstairs. We'll make our stand down here."

"Your stand?" Kay squeaked out as she turned in to her bedroom.

"If they're looking for the flash drive and Kaleb, they'll be coming inside. So far, we haven't heard any shots. That means they're taking—"

The glass in the window on the right wall of her bedroom shattered.

"I'll get Kaleb. Go into the hall."

She backpedaled, and her shoulder hit the side of the door frame as she went through. It barely registered when Drake approached, thrusting Kaleb into her arms.

"No time to get upstairs. Hide in the bathroom under the stairs. Don't leave until one of us comes for you. Go!" he said, turning away from her.

Gunfire erupted in her bedroom, prodding her to move as fast as she could in the dark. She trailed her hand along the wall, and when she came out into the back of the large entry hall, she veered to the left, feeling her way to the powder room under the stairs.

More shots sounded from the living room area, spurring her even faster. Kaleb whimpered and wiggled in her one-armed embrace.

"Shh, sweetie," she whispered in as soothing a voice as she could manage.

Probing the side of the staircase, she grazed her fingertips over a door frame. She couldn't remember if there was another door near the powder room. She grasped the knob and twisted and pulled it toward her. When she entered and took two steps, she ran into a counter and sink. After turning the lock, she sank to the floor and cuddled Kaleb close, rocking him to calm him while the sound of guns going off seemed to fill the whole house.

Eight men against three. The only thing she could think to do was pray.

As Drake reentered Kay's bedroom, a man dived through the broken window. Drake aimed his gun and shot the intruder as he tried to rise from the floor. A bullet whizzed by Drake, and he swiveled toward the window, where another guy stood. He fired at him while he dropped to the floor next to the bed.

He prayed Kay and Kaleb made it to the restroom. Since he'd been talking to Pierce on his cell phone when the power went out, Drake hoped the lieutenant figured something was wrong and sent help.

He peeked over the mattress and spied two men at the window. Both fired at him, and he dropped back down. He looked at the space beneath the bed and decided to crawl under it and see if he could surprise both attackers. He wiggled his way to the other side and peeked up at the window only a few feet away. When one man leaned sideways to look inside the room, Drake was tempted to shoot him, but that would give away where he was and he wanted both intruders.

The man stepped over the windowsill, quickly followed by his cohort. Drake sighted the first assailant and shot him. As he fell to the floor, Drake fired at the second guy. He went down, too. Drake scrambled from beneath the bed and hurried to check the three attackers' status. One was dead. The second one had a heartbeat but was bleeding out fast. The third lifted his weapon and squeezed the trigger.

The bullet struck Drake, and he faltered. As he went down, he fired his gun. His shoulder hit the floor. Pain streaked through his body.

When he tried to get up, the sound of a helicopter landing vied with the barrage of gunfire in the other parts of the house. He needed to help Dallas and Flynn, then find Kay and Kaleb before Soto got to them.

In the powder room Kay rocked Kaleb, hoping he would sleep. All the sounds bombarding her sent tremors through her. She had to remain composed or Kaleb would sense it and start crying.

Breathe deeply.

Think of something calm, peaceful.

An image of Drake filled her mind. The sensations his kiss created in her flowed through her, replacing the fear. She hadn't come this far to let Soto have Kaleb or the flash drive—to murder more people. She dug deep for the reservoir of courage she drew from when running into a burning building.

She leaned close to Kaleb's ear and softly sang "Silent Night." The song had helped him go to bed in the past days. She felt the tension draining from Kaleb—and her. Kaleb's head rolled to the side against her arm.

He was going to sleep in the midst of a war raging outside their door. She reclined against the cabinets, wishing she could, too. She closed her eyes, blocking the noise as much as possible.

Suddenly something crashed against the door. Then again and again.

A person?

No, something else.

On the fourth impact, the door crashed open. Who did it? It was too dark to see, but she heard a person breathing heavily, moving closer.

A large hand clamped around her arm and jerked her to her feet. Even before she was steady, Kaleb was wrenched from her embrace.

"No!" She clutched the counter behind her.

"He's my son!" Then to someone who must be near, a man's voice said, "Take him to the helicopter. I'll be there shortly." A couple of heartbeats later, he gripped her other arm, too. "I'm going to kill you like I did your sister."

The calm chill in Alejandro's voice unnerved her more than his hands digging into her flesh. He released one arm, but before she could react, his fingers encircled her throat, squeezing.

Blood streamed down Drake's left arm. Pain radiated through his body. He grabbed the end of a pillowcase and shook it loose from the pillow, then tied it around his wound as best he could. He didn't have time for anything else. Kay and Kaleb were in danger. No doubt the helicopter was Soto's doing, and he could be on it to make sure this assault worked.

Drake staggered out into the hallway and hurried as fast as he could to the restroom. He grasped his gun in his right hand, prepared to make a stand outside that room. When he came into the foyer, he quickly scanned his surroundings as he headed toward Kay's location. He rounded the staircase and spied the open door.

Gritting his teeth, he willed his body to keep moving. Kay was in trouble. Just inside the room, a man held Kay by her neck. She fought him, but her attacker held onto her.

"Let her go!"

The assailant glanced back at him through his own night-vision goggles. He couldn't tell if it was Soto or one of his cohorts. All he knew was the man was trying to kill Kay, his hands still about her neck. If he fired his gun, he might injure Kay.

"Now!" Drake moved closer, trying to find a better angle.

Kay's attacker swung around, using her as a human shield. Drake was an expert shot, but the conditions—only thermal vision and close quarters—would hamper his ability, especially as he felt his strength siphoning from him because of blood loss.

"She's coming with me." The guy dragged her into the foyer, her body still between them as he made his way toward the front door.

With his maneuvering, his hold must have loosened around Kay's neck, because she was no longer docile but striking out at him and trying to yank his hands away from her neck. Drake waited for any opportunity to take Soto out before he left the house. Kay would die if he managed to take her.

It was as if she heard his thoughts. The closer she came to the front door, the more she fought, kicking Soto wherever she could. Drake lifted his gun, stepping closer. The second she landed one debilitating hit with her knee, she broke free. Her assailant went down, and Drake rushed in, his gun pointed at the man's head.

A foot away, the guy lunged for Drake and his weapon. He wouldn't give it up. The attacker brought him down, wrestling for the gun. When it went off, the sound blasted through the foyer.

SIXTEEN

Kay entered the same hospital that had been evacuated two days ago and rode the elevator up to the third floor. Although her brother-in-law had been killed and the members of the *Muerte* Cartel operating in the United States rounded up by the DEA and Texas Rangers, Dallas accompanied her. The Mexican authorities were moving against the drug ring in their country, but even knowing that, Kay didn't feel totally safe. It was hard to forget the past couple of weeks—the death of her sister and the sight of Drake collapsing right after the gun went off in his struggle with Alejandro.

Drake had had surgery on his left arm yesterday. She'd been there beside him the day before while he recovered, but today she'd been tied up with the various law enforcement agencies working on the case. Then she'd filed for full custody of Kaleb, his nearest living relative in the United States. She'd been granted temporary custody in the meantime.

"I'll stay out here," Dallas said in the third-floor hallway. "He's been wondering where you were."

"You told him what I had to do?"

"Yes. But he said you two haven't really had a conversation, between the medication he was on and his family hovering around his bed."

That was what she'd been avoiding. She owed him so much. Especially this visit to say good-bye. She needed to disappear. She couldn't take a chance someone from the cartel would come after her—not with Kaleb.

She knocked, then opened the door and stepped into Drake's room.

He smiled as she walked toward the bed. "Where's Kaleb?"

"Anna is watching him, along with your dad and brother."

"You just missed Pierce. He left ten minutes ago after he filled me in on the wrap-up of the case. Have you talked to him today?"

"No. I did yesterday." She stopped at the right side of his bed.

He clasped her hand and tugged her even closer. "They're going to let me out later today."

"You just had surgery yesterday."

"And I'm doing well. Granted, I still have to

take it easy until the doctor clears me for duty again. I figure I'll be back by the first of the year, but that means I'll have time for us to get to know each other when bullets aren't flying."

She slipped her hand from his and backed away. "No, I can't stay here and put you in any more danger. You've saved me more than once."

"What are you talking about?" He carefully pushed himself up to a sitting position.

"I can't stay. What if the cartel comes after me?"

"The cartel has been rounded up. It was a new one pushing into the territories of other cartels. They never like that. They have been cooperating with the authorities to make sure no one is left to run it. There were people who gladly turned against Soto. He was ruthless and didn't care who he killed to get what he wanted. His philosophy was if you crossed him, your family was fair game, like in the case of the couple you saw killed in the stable."

She shook her head and turned for the door. "No, I can't take that chance."

Before she could clasp the knob and leave, Drake was behind her. He twisted her toward him. "If I've learned nothing else lately, it's that we have to enjoy the present and not worry about what could happen. We don't know what that will be."

She gestured toward his arm. "You took your IV out."

"That's because you were leaving. Come back in and sit with me. If I thought it was dangerous, I'd go with you and Kaleb. We can't live in fear." He combed his right hand through her hair, cupping the back of her head. "I love you. I never thought I would say that to another woman, but for the first time in years, I feel alive, renewed." He lowered his head toward hers, his lips whispering across hers as he murmured he loved her again.

She couldn't resist the words or him. She wound one arm around him, avoiding his left side, and deepened the kiss he'd started. In a short time, they had gone through a lot of trials and tribulations, but he was right. She couldn't push him away. "I love you," she murmured against his mouth.

Kay gently pushed him onto his hospital bed. "I'm calling your nurse. You need your IV hooked up, because I want you out of here as fast as possible. Christmas will be here before we know it. Kaleb's first one."

Drake snagged her hand near him. "Our first one as a couple."

At his family ranch, Drake sat on the couch in the den, relishing his family around him. Mandy, her husband and their four children had arrived yesterday, Christmas Eve, to spend a few days. His sister's ten-year-old daughter had doted on Kaleb since she came and made sure her siblings included Kaleb in everything. And the baby Drake had come to love cherished every moment in the middle of all the activities.

Kay, who was remembering more each day, entered the room with two mugs of hot chocolate. She made a beeline for him and took the seat next to him. "Sorry it took so long, but Anna needed some help with the Christmas dinner." She passed him his drink.

"I figured it was that or my sister was grilling you."

Kay laughed. "That was late last night when everyone else was asleep." Her smile grew. "I heard a lot about you."

"Don't believe everything she said."

"Which part should I forget? The time you saved a puppy caught in a barbed-wire fence or when you patiently showed her how to ride a horse?"

The heat of a blush seared his cheeks.

Kay leaned over and kissed the side of his face. "Her stories of you all growing up only confirmed what I already knew."

"I know we've opened all our Christmas presents, but I still have one more." He put his hot chocolate down, then rose and pulled her to her feet. Hands still clasped, he headed for the front porch, where he'd left the wrapped gift.

In these past weeks since El Paso, he'd had a lot of time to recuperate and think. He realized meeting Kay had changed his whole life. He no longer dwelled in the past. He'd let go of his hatred toward Shanna's killer. It was only hurting him. He looked forward to the present and future—he hoped with Kay and Kaleb.

Outside he picked up the box and gave it to her. Her eyes twinkled as she tore off the wrapping paper, then lifted the lid and stared at the piece of paper.

"I forgot all about this. When did you receive the DNA results?"

"A couple of days ago. Of course, we already knew what they would be, since you and Kassandra were twins. You are a parental match to Kaleb." He gestured toward the piece of paper. "Now it's official, which brings me to the second part of the gift."

He knelt in front of her and pulled out a small box. When he opened it to reveal a large square diamond surrounded with smaller ones, he said, "Kay—Kayden—Rollins, will you marry me? I want to be a husband to you and a father to Kaleb."

She went down on her knees and cradled his

face in her hands. "I love you. Yes, Kaleb and I will follow you anywhere you want to go."

Drake took the ring from the box and slipped it on Kay's left finger, then with his right arm, he drew her against him and kissed her with all the love he felt.

* * * * *

If you loved this exciting romantic suspense, pick up the first book in Margaret Daley's
LONE STAR JUSTICE *miniseries*
HIGH RISK REUNION

And be sure to check out
Margaret's previous miniseries
ALASKAN SEARCH AND RESCUE
THE YULETIDE RESCUE
TO SAVE HER CHILD
THE PROTECTOR'S MISSION
STANDOFF AT CHRISTMAS

Available now from
Love Inspired Suspense!

Find more great reads at
www.LoveInspired.com

Dear Reader,

Can you imagine waking up one day and you can't even recall your name? It would totally shake up your life from dealing with large issues to small ones. I think we tend to take for granted who we are and our memories. But what if all that was taken away from you?

In *Lone Star Christmas Rescue*, I explore what happens to a person when she doesn't remember who she is. Our personalities are formed by our past. Our experiences shape who we are. When Kay's memory is wiped away, she has to struggle to find herself. She doesn't know who to trust or how she ended up with amnesia. Even when she begins to remember bits and pieces of her previous life, she doesn't know if she will ever remember everything.

I love hearing from readers. You can contact me at margaretdaley@gmail.com or at P. O. Box 2074, Tulsa, OK 74101. You can also learn more about my books at http://www.margaretdaley. com. I have a monthly newsletter that you can sign up for on my website.

Best wishes,
Margaret

Get 2 Free Books,
Plus 2 Free Gifts—
just for trying the
Reader Service!

Get 2 Free Books,
Plus 2 Free Gifts—
just for trying the Reader Service!

READERSERVICE.COM

Manage your account online!

- Review your order history
- Manage your payments
- Update your address

> *We've designed the*
> *Reader Service website*
> *just for you.*

Enjoy all the features!

- Discover new series available to you, and read excerpts from any series.
- Respond to mailings and special monthly offers.
- Browse the Bonus Bucks catalog and online-only exculsives.
- Share your feedback.

Visit us at:
ReaderService.com